W9-BWV-106

On the count of fifty, the Executioner moved into action

Bolan came around the curve of the tunnel with the AKSU firing into the chamber's entrance. But he had to be somewhat cautious and reduce the risk of breaking the chemical flasks if they were in the room. The only way to do this was to hit hard, find direct targets and to strike with surprise, preventing the enemy from firing back and setting up a siege situation.

Unloading continuous rounds as he moved, Bolan finally got his first look at the place where the terrorists had made their base.

MACK BOLAN ®
The Executioner

#230 Deep Attack
#231 Slaughter Squad
#232 Jackal Hunt
#233 Tough Justice
#234 Target Command
#235 Plague Wind
#236 Vengeance Rising
#237 Hellfire Trigger
#238 Crimson Tide
#239 Hostile Proximity
#240 Devil's Guard
#241 Evil Reborn
#242 Doomsday Conspiracy
#243 Assault Reflex
#244 Judas Kill
#245 Virtual Destruction
#246 Blood of the Earth
#247 Black Dawn Rising
#248 Rolling Death
#249 Shadow Target
#250 Warning Shot
#251 Kill Radius
#252 Death Line
#253 Risk Factor
#254 Chill Effect
#255 War Bird
#256 Point of Impact
#257 Precision Play
#258 Target Lock
#259 Nightfire
#260 Dayhunt
#261 Dawnkill
#262 Trigger Point
#263 Skysniper
#264 Iron Fist
#265 Freedom Force
#266 Ultimate Price
#267 Invisible Invader
#268 Shattered Trust
#269 Shifting Shadows
#270 Judgment Day
#271 Cyberhunt
#272 Stealth Striker
#273 UForce
#274 Rogue Target
#275 Crossed Borders
#276 Leviathan
#277 Dirty Mission
#278 Triple Reverse
#279 Fire Wind
#280 Fear Rally
#281 Blood Stone
#282 Jungle Conflict
#283 Ring of Retaliation
#284 Devil's Army
#285 Final Strike
#286 Armageddon Exit
#287 Rogue Warrior
#288 Arctic Blast
#289 Vendetta Force
#290 Pursued
#291 Blood Trade
#292 Savage Game
#293 Death Merchants
#294 Scorpion Rising
#295 Hostile Alliance
#296 Nuclear Game
#297 Deadly Pursuit
#298 Final Play
#299 Dangerous Encounter
#300 Warrior's Requiem
#301 Blast Radius
#302 Shadow Search
#303 Sea of Terror
#304 Soviet Specter
#305 Point Position

The Executioner

Don Pendleton's

POINT POSITION

A GOLD EAGLE BOOK FROM

WORLDWIDE®

TORONTO • NEW YORK • LONDON
AMSTERDAM • PARIS • SYDNEY • HAMBURG
STOCKHOLM • ATHENS • TOKYO • MILAN
MADRID • WARSAW • BUDAPEST • AUCKLAND

If you purchased this book without a cover you should be aware that this book is stolen property. It was reported as "unsold and destroyed" to the publisher, and neither the author nor the publisher has received any payment for this "stripped book."

First edition April 2004
ISBN 0-373-64305-5

Special thanks and acknowledgment to
Andy Boot for his contribution to this work.

POINT POSITION

Copyright © 2004 by Worldwide Library.

All rights reserved. Except for use in any review, the reproduction or utilization of this work in whole or in part in any form by any electronic, mechanical or other means, now known or hereafter invented, including xerography, photocopying and recording, or in any information storage or retrieval system, is forbidden without the written permission of the publisher, Worldwide Library, 225 Duncan Mill Road, Don Mills, Ontario, Canada M3B 3K9.

All characters in this book have no existence outside the imagination of the author and have no relation whatsoever to anyone bearing the same name or names. They are not even distantly inspired by any individual known or unknown to the author, and all incidents are pure invention.

® and TM are trademarks of the publisher. Trademarks indicated with ® are registered in the United States Patent and Trademark Office, the Canadian Trade Marks Office and in other countries.

Printed in U.S.A.

The battle is not to the strong alone; it is to the vigilant, the active, the brave.

—Patrick Henry

Men rise from one ambition to another; first they seek to secure themselves from attack, and then they attack others.

—Niccolo Machiavelli

Every battle has a decisive moment—either forge ahead or go home. I'll play to the end every time.

—Mack Bolan

THE
MACK BOLAN®
LEGEND

Nothing less than a war could have fashioned the destiny of the man called Mack Bolan. Bolan earned the Executioner title in the jungle hell of Vietnam.

But this soldier also wore another name—Sergeant Mercy. He was so tagged because of the compassion he showed to wounded comrades-in-arms and Vietnamese civilians.

Mack Bolan's second tour of duty ended prematurely when he was given emergency leave to return home and bury his family, victims of the Mob. Then he declared a one-man war against the Mafia.

He confronted the Families head-on from coast to coast, and soon a hope of victory began to appear. But Bolan had broken society's every rule. That same society started gunning for this elusive warrior—to no avail.

So Bolan was offered amnesty to work within the system against terrorism. This time, as an employee of Uncle Sam, Bolan became Colonel John Phoenix. With a command center at Stony Man Farm in Virginia, he and his new allies—Able Team and Phoenix Force—waged relentless war on a new adversary: the KGB.

But when his one true love, April Rose, died at the hands of the Soviet terror machine, Bolan severed all ties with Establishment authority.

Now, after a lengthy lone-wolf struggle and much soul-searching, the Executioner has agreed to enter an "arm's-length" alliance with his government once more, reserving the right to pursue personal missions in his Everlasting War.

1

"That's it. The one on the left," the bearded man whispered to his two companions.

The small woman to his left shot him a quizzical look. "You sure about that, Jean-Louis?"

The bearded man—Jean-Louis Garrault—shrugged in a manner that could be taken as almost parodic, given his French nationality. But then, the idea of being a French national was something that would have made Garrault spit blood in anger.

"What the hell does that mean, Jean-Louis?" asked the squat, ugly man to his right. "It either is or it isn't."

"Of course it is, you idiot," Garrault muttered angrily. "Do you really think I would direct us to the wrong target?"

"Of course, you wouldn't," the squat man replied. "I do, however, know that you are far from perfect."

There was an angry, tense silence as Garrault stared down at the shorter man. Salvatore Signella was a Sicilian, a man who had no apparent fight with the French government and yet had joined Garrault, Francine Malpas—the woman to Garrault's left—and the other members of Destiny's Spear, a direct action political cell—with just the comment that his political views were in sympathy with theirs. The fact that he had joined at the time they had first gained the patronage of Hector Chavez-Smith had a significance that wasn't lost on Garrault. But, like the others, he ignored this because of the cash that Chavez-Smith poured into their organization, enabling them to carry out their campaign of action.

It was just that on nights like this, it seemed that they were more a vehicle for Chavez-Smith than an autonomous cell in their own right. It was the Chilean drug baron who had wanted them to make this snatch, and it seemed to serve no obvious political purpose. It wouldn't even—as Garrault understood matters—get them into the media in the same way that their bank raids to raise funds had done in the past. To take the money from the pigs was the best way to make them aware of their sick status in the corrupt system, Garrault thought. But this?

Signella met the Frenchman's stare and returned one that was stony and impassive. He was unblinking. There was no way that the Frenchman could read what was going on behind those blank eyes. All he knew was that he was strong— lean and wiry, with a good four inches in height over the Sicilian—but that Signella was more powerful, with muscles like cords on his neck and forearms. The Sicilian also had an almost offhand callousness and disregard for pain that made Garrault shudder when he considered going one-on-one.

So he was glad when Malpas stepped between them.

"Stop this pissing contest," she murmured coldly. "If you're sure that's the target, then we've got work to do."

It gave Garrault no pleasure in the fact that Signella looked away first. It was an offhand gesture that suggested Malpas was right, and that Garrault was foolish to continue.

The target sat about four hundred yards from where they

stood under cover. It was a fuel tanker, parked between two others that were identical in model and with the same name and logo on the sides, differentiated only by the amount of mud, dust and grime that covered each vehicle.

The tankers were situated in a position where abduction would be easily noticed.

"Guards?" Signella growled, gesturing with the muzzle of his Uzi at the five men who were spread across the yard. Two were sitting on upturned metal barrels, talking. Another was checking a toolbox by a rickety wooden shed. The final two were at separate ends of the yard. One seemed to be urinating through the chain-link fence, and the other was surreptitiously smoking, in blatant disregard for the sign above his head.

Five to three, and spread out. This wouldn't be easy. Garrault felt the pit of his stomach begin to ripple with fear and excitement, as it did before any mission.

"They don't look like they are," he replied in a voice that was too calm for his current state, "but we have to assume so. If this is as important as Hector believes, then it would be guarded. There is no one else in the yard, right, Francine?" He paused and looked across to the woman, whose task it had been to do a recon earlier. When she assented, he continued. "Then we have to assume they are hostile and take them out as quickly as possible."

Signella grunted. "Let's do it, then."

The trio of Destiny's Spear gunners—or, as the French government designated them, three members of one of the most wanted and dangerous right-wing terrorist splinter groups currently in operation—moved out. Despite any personal antipathies, they were committed to their cause, to the extent of undergoing rigorous training, and so moved with a stealth and skill that ranked them with the best of terrorists.

The yard where the three tankers rested was in the middle of the port area of Marseilles. A half mile down the road lay the bright lights and easy life of the millionaires' playground, where jet-setters berthed their yachts and walked the brightly lit streets with the beautiful people who stayed within that small area. But there was also nocturnal activity of a vastly differing nature. The majority of business in the port area was conducted by day, but there were also columns of strong arc lights that enabled loading and unloading to continue in the hours of darkness. Container boats, cargo ships and freighters of all descriptions—and of all kinds of manifests, with few questions asked for a few francs in hand—used the port, and there were always seamen along the walkways and paths between the water and the cargo sheds.

In the yards—little more than flat-packed dirt or loose gravel squares with makeshift sheds and trailers for offices—the container trucks and tankers were berthed when not in use, hired out by haulage firms by the month. Because of this, security was at a minimum, with chain-link fencing and padlocked gates seemingly the extent of any precautions taken by those who leased the land. The area was lit at night by fading halogen lamps mounted poorly in the corners, leaving inviting pools of shadow.

It was in these shadows that the three terrorists moved. Although it was quiet at this end of the docks, there was still enough distant background noise to mask their progress if they moved stealthily. They had trained to do this, all of them having traveled to the United States to train in camps run by paramilitary right-wing groups who had affiliations with other groups in Europe, Africa and Asia.

Signella moved off to the right, flanking the two men on barrels, and heading for the man who was apparently urinating. In a distant corner, with his back to the main body of the yard, his hands hidden from view by his actions, the guard presented the greatest potential threat. He was the unknown factor, as all the other men had their hands in view. None had weapons, and the fractions of seconds it would take them to draw represented an advantage for the terrorists. Outnumbered as they were, this could only be a good thing.

The Sicilian palmed a leaf-bladed knife from his shirt, feeling the balance of the shaft and hilt in the hollow of his hand. Even in the almost nonexistent light of the yard, the blade gleamed. He looked up, judging the distance between himself and the guard with his back to him. In truth, the man could have been little more than an unsuspecting mechanic taking a leak at an inopportune moment. It was of no account to the Sicilian, who raised his arm and threw the knife in a fluid motion. It had power and precision, and it had a blade of razor-sharpened Toledo steel that bit into flesh, ripping easily through cloth. The man at the chain-link fence pitched forward, the fencing sagging slightly on old posts as it took his weight. His hands fell free, his bladder continuing to empty down his lifeless legs as he slumped to the dirt.

Signella looked around sharply. The man had made little noise in dying, but still enough to be noticed. He raised the Uzi, ready.

A thin smile crossed his lips as the sudden explosion of action showed that he had no need to worry.

FRANCINE MALPAS MOVED toward the smoking man in the far corner. Like Signella, she was shielded partly from view by the shadows of the malfunctioning halogen lights, and partly by the containers that were stacked by the gates, three across and two high. They were old and rusting, and seemed to have been there from some previous leasee who hadn't bothered to remove them when his lease ran out.

Strange, she thought. If this was a military operation, it was negligent that the containers be left to provide cover for any enemy…unless, perhaps, removing them would have drawn too much attention to the new occupants of the yard. No matter, it gave her that extra cover she needed.

The female terrorist was no expert with knives. She preferred to take out her targets with lead. To this end, she was carrying an AKSU assault rifle, which had the power of an old Kalashnikov, but was much easier to conceal and carry as it had a folding stock and shortened muzzle. It was, however, just as accurate.

The smoking man was, as she could tell the closer she drew, actually only in a pose of relaxation. In truth, he was sharp-eyed, one hand always hovering near the pocket of his oil-stained blue coveralls.

Garrault had been right after all. They were on guard, and this had to be the right target.

She could see the shape of a long-barreled revolver beneath the baggy coveralls. Probably a .357 Magnum Colt Python, not the sort of firearm that was preferred by the U.S. military, but probably the personal preference of an undercover security operative.

She felt a shiver of sexual excitement run through her as she raised the AKSU, sighted her target and tapped the trigger. A blast of three armored shells ripped into the man's chest and stomach, the rippling internal damage taking his life if the shells themselves did not.

She had no idea how the others were doing with their targets. However, now she had broken the silence, all hell would break loose.

GARRAULT HAD the hardest of the initial targets. He had to take out the two men on the barrels and cover the man at the shed. There was enough distance between the two groups to make it impossible to take them with one swift arc of gunfire, and so he had to make a choice. Would he hit the group of two and knock out the greater number, or would he take the man by the shed, who was the only one of the guards with anything approaching cover?

Considering he was still in good cover himself, and not under immediate threat from the two men in the open, he opted for the man by the shed. An enemy in cover could cost them valuable time in taking the tanker.

Garrault was carrying a Heckler & Koch MP-5, one of the most reliable SMGs on the market. Once, a jamming Uzi had nearly cost him his life, and it had been Malpas who had saved him. He never wanted to be in anyone's debt—particularly hers—ever again. From that day, he had refused to carry an Uzi. It was almost a fetish, but it gave him an added confidence to be carrying an MP-5, a confidence that was reflected in the manner in which he took aim with an almost casual ease, not hurrying his fire. A gentle tap on the trigger, and a quick burst of rounds cut into the man standing by the shed, still looking over his toolbox. It was a sound echoed by the blast of the AKSU, and the two men in the middle were momentarily torn between the two bursts of fire as Garrault's target sprawled across the earth, staining the dirt with his blood and noisily emptying the contents of his toolbox across his descending path.

The momentary hesitation between targets cost the two men their lives. As they reached into their coveralls, withdrawing Browning Hi-Power pistols, which were completely inadequate against SMG fire from cover, they wavered between the two directions of fire, leaving them completely unprepared for gunfire from yet another source.

Signella had turned after hearing the burst of autofire from the far end of the yard, and broke cover, firing with a spray 'n'pray motion as he ran. The Uzi chattered a stream of rounds that cut into the two security men at waist level, tearing through the muscle and spinal cord below the ribs and above the pelvis, taking the softest and most vulnerable areas of flesh.

It was short, violent and effective. Almost severed in two, both men dropped to the ground.

"Take the tanker, quickly," Signella yelled, turning on his heel to double back toward the security man he had killed with the leaf-bladed knife.

"You sure it's the center tanker?" Malpas asked as she and Garrault reached the vehicles.

"Hundred percent," he snapped with a touch of acerbity. He didn't like the note of doubt in her voice. She was always like that when she had just killed.

The tanker doors were unlocked, and as soon as they were in the cab, Garrault broke the casing under the steering column and hot-wired the engine. It spluttered and grunted into life, sounding sluggish.

"Hurry up, we don't have much time," Malpas snapped.

"You think I don't know that?" Garrault muttered peevishly. "Where is that Sicilian bastard? He's supposed to be on the gate."

As he spoke, he turned the tanker in the enclosed space of

the yard and headed toward the gates, which were still locked. They had made their way through the chain-link fencing with bolt cutters, having checked for alarm wiring, and were relying on the Sicilian to cut the padlock on the gates.

"Shit, why'd he go back?" Garrault asked as he slowed the truck before the locked gates. He listened desperately over the sound of the engine for any sirens. It was unlikely that the brief bursts of gunfire would be heard over the sound of the docks, even this late. The yards were too isolated for it to carry that far. But he didn't want to draw any more attention by having to charge the gates or drive the tanker through the city with the front of the grille damaged.

Just as his patience was wearing thin enough for him to gun the engine and make for the gates, Signella came loping into view. He took the bolt cutters from his belt and sliced through the chain attached to the padlock, pushing the doors open one at a time. He ran back to the truck, panting heavily as he climbed up through the open passenger-side door.

"You took your time," Malpas gritted as the Sicilian pulled the door shut behind him.

"Got my first man with a knife," he panted. "Unique blade, made myself. Too identifiable."

"Should have shot the bastard and saved us some time," Garrault muttered as he swung the truck out of the gate and onto the dockside road that led toward the center of Marseilles.

All three of the terrorists kept a close watch as they left the docks behind and entered the still busy night. They thundered past the harbor where the expensive yachts lay moored, and up into the poorer district before hitting the road leading out of Marseilles.

"Think Chavez-Smith was watching us pass?" Malpas

mused as they hit the main road without incident, and they all felt able to relax a little.

"Nothing would surprise me," Garrault replied as he took the second exit, navigating a series of small country roads until they saw a darkened sedan in the middle of a field. As they drew near, the vehicle's lights flicked on.

"Good. Emil's ready," Signella announced as the tanker slowed to a halt.

"You know for sure where it is in here?" Malpas asked the Sicilian as they climbed down.

"If Hector is right, and there's no reason to doubt it," he said with a sideways glance at Garrault, "then it should be under here." He disappeared beneath the tanker. "Light," he snapped from beneath.

Emil Herve came forward with a flashlight, bending to shine it under the chassis. He was a lean, dark man with his black hair in a ponytail. The light reflected onto his sharp features.

Signella pulled off a section of casing that should have housed the braking system.

"Got it," he whispered triumphantly. He pulled out a small wrapped parcel that he handed to Herve before replacing the casing.

"This is it?" the man asked with disbelief. "They use something this big to hide this?"

"Moron, no one is supposed to know how big this thing is. That's why we've taken the whole tanker and lost it out here. We want them to think we don't have it yet, maybe don't know exactly what we're looking for. Time is of the essence, and all we can grab we must take. Now let's get out of here and back to base."

They piled into the sedan, and Herve turned it to head back to the main road.

Throughout the operation, all four terrorists had been wearing latex gloves. But Signella hadn't realized that the left index finger had ripped while he replaced the plastic chassis casing.

2

The man known as the Executioner was enjoying a much needed rest at the ultracovert Stony Man Farm. Although, in the case of Mack Bolan, a much needed rest entailed the kind of routine that would exhaust many men. For the best part of a week he had been between missions, and had spent the days sharpening his skills and reflexes. The firearms range had seen a vast amount of ammo expended as he honed his marksmanship and speed. The gym had seen him put in a large number of hours training, both in basic weight, muscle and bodybuilding, and also in unarmed combat and the various branches of martial arts in which he had knowledge—a knowledge that had left his sparring partners wishing they had stayed in bed.

In between the physical training, Bolan took the time to hone his computer skills.

That just left the evenings for Bolan to wind down. Most of his life was spent living on adrenaline, at the knife edge of action. And, if he was honest with himself, he would admit that his War Everlasting had left him as something of an adrenaline junkie. Relaxing was something that didn't come easily to him.

Which was where Barbara Price entered the picture. As mission controller, the tall honey-blonde was a vital part of the Stony Man machine, and even Aaron Kurtzman, in his more mellow moments, would admit that it would be hard to run the place without her analytical skills and technological expertise. She had also proved herself as a hell of a fighter.

Despite everything, at the end of the long day there lurked, beneath the hardened battle shell of the solider, a human being. He still cared passionately about those people who lived and fought alongside him, would spill his own blood rather than see theirs spilt. People like Jack Grimaldi. And although the battle-hardened pilot knew the risks he ran, Bolan would still take the risks himself rather than see his friend killed.

Barbara Price was a different matter altogether. Bolan knew what she felt for him, although she kept it to herself. They both knew their work came first. But when they could, they tried to find some quiet time together.

THE SHARP AND INSISTENT ringing of the phone by the bedside woke the soldier instantly from his sleep. Pausing only to allow his head to clear, and to disentangle his right arm from underneath the stirring, naked form of Barbara Price, Bolan reached across and picked up the handset. By the time it was at his ear, he was fully awake. The voice of Hal Brognola cut into the morning with no preamble.

"I need you in the War Room in fifteen. Something nasty's gone down in France, and it needs immediate attention…and tell Barbara we'll need her, too," the director of the Sensitive Operations Group added.

"Okay," the soldier replied briefly, replacing the receiver and rising from the bed.

Price opened her eyes and blinked, taking in Bolan's tautly muscled form as he padded toward the bathroom.

"Trouble?"

"Yeah." He looked over his shoulder. "Hal needs us both in the War Room in fifteen."

They both arrived in the War Room ten minutes later.

"Coffee?" Aaron Kurtzman asked as they entered the room.

"Not if it's your usual acid brew, Aaron," Price said, shuddering.

"It isn't," Kurtzman growled. "Hal made sure of that."

"Right. I don't want anyone getting a caffeine high from that brew while I'm trying to brief them," the head Fed replied.

Bolan joined Kurtzman at the side-table and poured coffee for himself and Price. "I'm wondering, Bear," he began, maintaining an innocent tone, "is that much caffeine in one cup actually a legal drug?"

"Very funny," the computer expert replied. "But I think you'll be wanting some of it when you've heard what we've got to say."

"Then let's begin," Bolan said, slipping back into his usual business tone, and handing the coffee to Price.

"First, I just downloaded this and I want you to watch it," Brognola began, tapping on a keyboard and bringing up footage on an enlarged monitor along one wall.

They watched in silence as the computer played French news footage of the raid on the dockside tanker yard, showing the break-in and the five corpses. It then cut to the tanker, left abandoned in the country by an open field.

Bolan's French was conversational rather than academic, so he had no trouble understanding the commentary. The

French media believed the gendarmerie to be baffled by the incident, as five men were murdered for the theft of an empty tanker. They put it down to a war between two haulage companies that was getting out of hand.

The footage finished.

"But it's more than that, right? Otherwise you wouldn't have got me out of bed. Not for some kind of Teamster war."

"You're right," Brognola replied. "Anything strike you as odd?"

"Yeah. Five men killed for one tanker. No damage to the other two. The fact that the tanker was then dumped…like they were looking for something. And it was a very professional hit. In and out, five men down and no casualties or sign of injuries on their side. I'd say that they were looking for something, and it had to do with that particular vehicle. One other thing. It said that four were shot, the fifth was killed by a knife wound, but that the knife was missing. Maybe it was easier to identify than any bullet or shell would be. To remove it from the body suggests someone who really knew what they were doing."

"There is one important thing they didn't say on the news report," Brognola said softly. "The five dead were all U.S. citizens, three being ex-Marines. And they were all armed. These people were good, but—"

"But what were they doing in a yard in Marseilles docks, heavily armed?" Bolan finished. "That question certainly needs answering."

Price nodded. "The other thing that gets alarms ringing is that the whole hit and lift was too clean—no prints?"

Kurtzman wagged a finger at her. "Now there's one of the most interesting things of all. We've managed to monitor a few communiqués between the path labs and the investigating officers, and it seems that these were very professional people. They used latex gloves, and there were no traces of prints, except..."

"Come on, Aaron, don't string us along. Cut to the chase," Price commented good-humoredly when Kurtzman paused for dramatic effect.

"Okay." Kurtzman smiled. "For a reason I can only speculate on, they removed part of the chassis casing that should have housed brake cables. But it didn't. They'd been rerouted, and this housed nothing more than a gap, where something could be concealed. When replacing the casing, one of the gang members tore the index finger of one glove—they found residual traces of latex—and left a nice, clear print behind."

"I take it this is where it gets interesting," Bolan said.

"It does," Brognola replied. The head Fed took up the story. "We've got the print. We've got an ID, and we've also got a file on the owner of that print."

Kurtzman punched the keyboard, and a photograph and printed information of birth, education, description, prison record, and political and criminal activities came up on the monitor.

"Salvatore Signella," Bolan murmured as he perused the information on screen. "Trained soldier, mercenary in Rwanda and Bosnia, seen action all over the globe. Last known to be working as a bodyguard for Hector Chavez-Smith, a Chilean drug baron who's expanded into arms. Pretty good at it, from what I hear. Then the certainties run out about ten months ago. Not known if he's still alive. Well, we know now. Because of his political sympathies and right-wing leanings, it's believed that he may have joined Destiny's Spear, a French terrorist organization with a known base in Marseilles. Hell, that'd figure. They're right on the spot for the hijacking, and they have links with right-wing organizations both in Europe, the UK and over here. They're being bankrolled by someone, but no one knows who. There have been several high-profile assassinations and robberies. But this change in MO is interesting."

The soldier turned to Brognola. "So why are they hijacking an empty tanker? What was in the hollowed-out space beneath the chassis? And why were there five armed Americans on the French docks?"

"You are, of course, assuming that it was the terrorist group behind this," Kurtzman commented.

"I know there's nothing definite, but as a working theory it fits so far. So why do I think that you're going to confirm it for me?"

"I was talking to the Oval Office earlier," Brognola said wearily, "and it gets complicated, Striker."

"It's never anything else," Bolan replied.

"The first thing is that the hidden space beneath the tanker chassis was being used to transport a number of chemical weapons to a rendezvous in Paris. They were coming up from Italy, via Marseilles. There's been a security leak, and the idea was to take an old and roundabout route and hide in plain sight."

"What are we talking here?" Bolan asked.

"Three vials of a newly developed compound, secured in a flask. Prototypes for secondary testing. It's an odorless, colorless vapor when mixed. Spreads on the air, and only needs one hundred-thousandth per liter of air to be effective. Allegedly, it breaks down in the body and leaves no traces, either. There's a certain Middle Eastern power, at war with his neighbors, who has expressed an interest in acquiring this. And we know that Chavez-Smith is dealing with this man."

"Makes a whole lot of sense so far. So you want me to go in and get the flask back while neutralizing the terrorists, right?" And when Brognola nodded, Bolan added, "But you said the first thing...so what's the complication?"

Kurtzman sighed. "Rumor—and it's strong enough to be a little more than a rumor—says that there was more than the flask being taken by this route. There have been whispers of a black project along the lines of sonic warfare."

"Sonic weapons are no secret. What's so special about this black project?" Bolan queried.

"Most sonic weapons go for frequency responses that can affect the bodily functions or impair the ability to think by blowing out the eardrums and causing brain damage. They're still not that subtle. Their idea of subtle is to disrupt thought patterns and cause confusion."

"But this baby is better than that, right?"

"This one is a real little bundle of joy," Kurtzman said. "It can be set to any number or combination of frequencies, and can cause anything from paralysis to complete enslavement."

"How is that possible?" Bolan asked.

"I did a little checking when Hal told me about this, as it stirred up a few memories. Over the past five years, a number of scientists have either gone missing or have been reported dead in accidents, the recovered bodies unidentifiable. They had one thing in common—they were all working on projects that had sonic warfare as their target field. What are the odds that they're not dead, but that they've been working on this? As far as I can figure, sonic weaponry would work on the principle of a kind of hypnosis, suppressing some brain waves but stimulating others that made someone particularly susceptible to suggestion."

Bolan whistled. "That's a hell of a double whammy if it's

been snatched. What does the President have to say on the matter?"

Brognola scowled. "It wasn't mentioned to me, and when I brought it up, the matter was denied flat out. What I can't figure is whether that was a denial because no one is supposed to know about the sonic weapons or a denial because they don't have the faintest idea what's been going on. They only know about the chemical weapons."

"The Man has never sold us out on anything that's been known before," Bolan commented. "I don't see why he would now, not after he's requested—I'm assuming that's my mission—I go after the chemical weapons."

"I'd like to think so," Brognola said quietly. "But if we're not supposed to know, or it's so black it's been hidden even from the Oval Office—which wouldn't be the first or last time, let's face it—then you know what it means?"

"Incoming from all sides," Bolan replied. "If we're out for the chemicals, then someone will be on the trail of the sonics. And whoever it is, they're sure as hell not going to be pleased to have me around."

"Maybe you should have an assist," Price suggested. She had remained silent for some time, taking in the situation. "Able Team is on a mission, but I could call some of Phoenix Force."

Bolan shook his head. "No, I figure you're right, but I'll only need one man, ready to come in at a moment's notice. Marseilles isn't that big, but there's a lot of action. If Destiny's Spear is based there, and have the area under tight security, a whole lot of heavies showing up are just going to scare them away. It'll be enough to just have me and maybe someone from the black-ops team stirring up the nest."

"I'll get Jack briefed then," Price stated.

Bolan grinned. "How d'you figure I'd want him?"

She shook her head. "There's no one else who can get in and out of situations better than a chopper pilot like Jack."

"I'll also need whatever we know about Destiny's Spear and this Chavez-Smith guy before I get equipped and ship out. Any background you've got."

Kurtzman smiled and tapped up a file from the computer. "I knew you'd ask, so we got it ready for you."

Bolan was already immersed in Kurtzman's briefing as Price left the room in search of Jack Grimaldi.

3

From Stony Man Farm in Virginia to Marseilles was a trip that took less than half the time it would have if the soldier had been forced to use a commercial airline. As it was, Jack Grimaldi piloted an Air Force transporter to a U.S. air base in northern France, and they commandeered a chopper to take them to Marseilles, landing at a small airfield outside the city. The Air Force plane and chopper had been ordered up by Hal Brognola, with Bolan traveling under the name of Colonel Brandon Stone. His military alias and the clearance that the big Fed was able to conjure up made for a smooth journey.

It was early evening when they arrived at the small airfield, and less than forty-eight hours since the tanker had been stolen and the chemical and sonic weapons taken. There was no way that Bolan could have been briefed and made the journey in a quicker time, but still he was worried that the trail would be too cold.

"Relax, Sarge," Grimaldi said as he touched down and killed the engine, the rotor of the chopper descending in tone from a whine to a deep and rhythmic whump as it slowed. "Another half hour or hour isn't going to make any difference."

"It may, Jack. Those weapons may already be on their way out of France."

"Easy, Sarge. Intel have said that Hector Chavez-Smith was having a little party tonight. That doesn't sound like the actions of a man who's about to run, does it?"

"No, it doesn't," Bolan agreed. "But it may not be Chavez-Smith who's taking the weapons out."

"Come on, you didn't even convince yourself with that," Grimaldi said, laughing. "What we know of that scumbag, he's going to want to see the color of the money in his own sweaty little hands before he hands them over to anyone. Which is why you want to crash his party, right?"

"You know me too well, Jack." Bolan smiled. "I figure that he's going to keep them on hand if he can. So if I can get on that boat, then maybe I can get them back and neutralize him at the same time. Then we can clean up his private army."

"Glad you said 'we' there, Sarge. How do I figure in this?"

"Right now, I want you to rest up and wait here. I'll keep a wire open at all times, and I want you to be ready to come in for a pickup when the action starts."

"Okay," Grimaldi agreed. "Before that, we need to get the local boys on side," he said, indicating an Air Force officer who was making his way from the small control tower building of the airfield to where the chopper was parked.

Bolan was out of the cockpit and halfway toward the young man before Grimaldi had dismounted.

"Sir, Lieutenant Frank Walters. I'm your liaison, Colonel," he snapped, coming to attention and saluting.

Bolan returned the salute and held out his hand.

The officer took the proffered hand and felt Bolan's iron-hard grip.

"Okay, Walters. Now, I take it you know we've flown down here on a covert operation and that you are to assist me and my partner in any way possible. Do you know what that mission is?"

"No, sir. All I know is what you've just reiterated," Walters said.

Bolan nodded. "That's good. This is strictly need-to-know. My compatriot and I plan to go in, hit hard and get the hell out. There should be no fallout in the direction of the American forces if we do our job. And if we don't, there will be no acceptance of responsibility. What you need to do is make sure that whatever I or Sergeant Galloway ask for," he added, using Grimaldi's cover for the mission, "is in place immediately. Right now, that means the chopper is refueled and maintained, and that the sergeant has a place to wait and monitor me in peace and comfort."

"That's no problem, sir," Walters replied.

"Good. I will need a car to use, preferably something inconspicuous for these regions. And I need briefing on the layout of the harbor area."

"I figured you might, Colonel Stone. I have a Citroën ready with a full tank of gas, and there are maps of the harbor area and coffee waiting. I've spent some time in the area on vacation, which is why my commanding officer made me your liaison. And—" he hesitated "—chew me out if I've overstepped, sir, but as we have been given no information about your evac plans at the end of mission, I've taken the liberty of getting clearance for an open-ended takeoff, and also making sure there will be a team on standby back at the base for as long as they are needed."

"That's good work."

Within a half hour, Bolan was headed into the heart of Marseilles in the Citroën supplied by his liaison. The combat bag was stowed in the trunk of the car, and he was wearing a loose shirt and khaki pants over his blacksuit. He was unwilling to discard the blacksuit and harness, as he planned for this to be a quick operation, and he wanted the armament fixed to the combat harness to be ready to hand.

He navigated the vehicle through the dense early evening traffic, where the French sense of driving meant that cars cut in front of one another with little regard for lanes or even direction of flow, slowed only by near collision, or the ranks of cyclists and motorcyclists who treated the cars as a moving slalom course. Added to this was the chaos of groups of pedestrians who seemed not even to notice the cars, but walked in front of the traffic as though their mass made them invincible.

And the heat was oppressive. As he sat in the car, Bolan felt prickles of perspiration gather under the blacksuit, despite the fact that it was made to insulate against heat as well as cold.

Taking the opportunity when it arose, he swung the car off the main road and down a narrow, cobbled side street where the pavement teemed with people lining up to gain admittance to a club he remembered from a previous visit. It was known in the area for being on the site of an old sewing machine factory, and the club owners commemorated this by having heavy old sewing machines attached to the tables. Attached by heavy bolts, they would have made formidable weapons in a bar brawl unless otherwise secured. Like most of the clubs in this quarter, the inside was dingy and oppressive, heavy with the scent of human sweat and alcohol. These places had never heard of air conditioning, and the lighting was minimal. As for fire regulations and restrictions on capacity, the owners would profess no knowledge of those things simply with a shrug.

Leaning heavily on the vehicle's horn, Bolan nosed slowly through the bottleneck of humanity around the club. He was glad when he was able to step on the gas, having parted the throng and emerged into the small square at the bottom of the road. He cut across and continued downhill on the road that brought him to the harbor, and the main drag parallel to the sea that serviced the millionaires' paradise.

The delineation between the two halves of Marseilles was sharp. One moment he was in a quarter where any kind of crime or vice was possible in the blink of an eye, where he could buy guns, drugs and women at cut prices. But by turning another corner he was in an area where there were women no money could buy. Despite the nominal presence of the gendarmerie, the thing that caught the soldier's eye was the large number of private security on display. Not that they were ostentatious. These were highly trained—and highly paid—professionals who were discreet, wearing clothes that were as beautifully cut as their employers', and that were able to disguise the bulges of concealed weapons necessary for the rich to feel safe. It was only Bolan's highly trained eye that singled them out.

A Porsche pulled out of a parking space along the side of the harbor road, and Bolan slid into the vacant slot quickly. The Citroën seemed too downmarket, too noticeable among the Mercedes, Ferraris and Porsches in the area, but it was too late to worry about that now. He had to move quickly.

And he knew exactly where he had to go. A stream of people moved toward a yacht that blared seventies funk music and was illuminated by searchlights bright enough to keep most of the poorer quarters lit for a week.

The heavy volume of guests making their way to the party would be both a hindrance and a help. It would make it easier for the soldier to hide among them, yet at the same time it would make combat difficult when the time came for action. The vast majority of these people were rich through legitimate means, and they were the very people he had sworn to protect in his War Everlasting. Somehow, he would have to find a way to wage war with the minimum of danger to these innocents.

But right now, that was unimportant. The immediate objective was to get on the yacht and confront Chavez-Smith.

As he moved onto the sidewalk and began to thread his way through the crowds, moving at a faster pace, he kept his attention focused on the security. Those nearest the parked Citroën had taken notice of him, the car being so out of place in this environment. They wore earpieces and had throat mikes, and Bolan could see them communicate with one another. That would mean he was expected. There was nothing to mark him out as dangerous, but he was seen as suspicious.

Drawing near the yacht, he could see that his description had been passed along the ranks as he noted several heavies trying to locate him. He was in luck that baggy pants and loose shirts seemed to be almost de rigueur with the jet set this season, and in this weather, as there were several men in the crowd dressed similarly enough to enable him to blend in a little more. The scanning heads of the security teams were confused by the numbers, and unable to single him out.

So far, so good. He joined the stream of partygoers that

was headed down the boardwalk toward the yacht that was the center of the action. More security was in evidence, and it was getting harder to stay anonymous. Up ahead, he could see the ramp leading onto the yacht, with the stream of partygoers on and off held up by security checks. Chavez-Smith had issued invitations, and crashers were being turned away.

As Bolan watched, one young couple began to argue with the security at the head of the entrance. They were in their early twenties, and looked rich but were dressed down. The young man had a mass of red curls that flopped angrily in the night breeze as he raised his voice and gesticulated at the security. Bolan could almost hear him saying "Don't you know who I am?" as he prodded the security man in the chest, while his companion encouraged him. She had blond hair and a dress that clung, but an unpleasant haughtiness that was obvious even at Bolan's distance.

Finally, the repeated refusals and the scorn of his companion forced the young man to action. He drew back his fist and aimed a punch at the security guard. It was stupid. The guard was twice his size and trained for such things. He caught the young man's fist in one large hand and squeezed. Bolan saw the young man fall to his knees, his scream of agony cutting through the night air. The guard then released his grip and lifted the young man up by his hair. When his face was level with the guard's shoulder, a short jab from his huge fist sent the young man flying backward down the ramp, onto the boardwalk, where excited partygoers had moved back to avoid being soiled by such action.

The haughtiness dropped from the young woman as she screeched and flew at the guard who had just laid out her man. She didn't get anywhere. She found herself lifted off her feet by the other guard at the entrance to the party. Having stood back while his partner dealt with the problem, he had been forgotten. Now he took her slim waist in his hands, almost encircling her with his grip, and lifted her off her feet. Her legs wheeled in the air with less grace than she would have wished before he put her over the side of the ramp and let her drop into the harbor.

"That should cool the bitch off a little," said a cool and cynical voice beside Bolan.

The soldier turned his head to take in a vision of beauty that was marred only by the signs that it was assisted a little by surgery. The woman standing beside him, watching the action, was Ethiopian. She had that swallowlike grace that only comes from that part of Africa. The surgery showed only in the contour beneath one eye, which was slightly too perfect. Not cosmetic. Bolan guessed it was reconstructive after an accident of some sort.

She smiled, but not with her eyes. "I know, my sweet. They can never get it as right as nature. But if one will drive a Ferrari a tad too fast, then one cannot complain. At least I am still alive and able to enjoy my life. My poor late husband was not so lucky."

"I'm sorry, I didn't mean to stare," Bolan said graciously.

"That's all right, my dear. You're up too close not to. Perhaps closer still if I'm lucky later?"

Bolan shrugged. "I doubt it. I wanted to get into the party—everyone in Marseilles does by the look of it—but I don't have an invite."

"Well, my little sweet, it just may be your lucky night. Perhaps mine as well. For you shall go to the ball, Cinderella. I have an invitation. For myself and an escort."

"And a beautiful woman like you doesn't have an escort?"

"Oh, yes, but he's still fussing over his Rolls-Royce, and

he's such a bore. Fuck him, darling, I've found someone much more interesting." She extended an elegant hand, which Bolan took and kissed. "I'm Countess Marie D'Orsini. Who are you?"

"Matt Cooper," Bolan replied, using a cover name. "At your service."

"Then I command we go and party hearty," she said with a smile.

Bolan was relieved. He wanted to do a recon without having to be on the offensive. And it was, it had to be admitted, a pleasure to cut through the crowd with such a beautiful woman on his arm. The people in front of them parted as they approached, and the countess was greeted and admired from all sides. Obviously, the woman was something of a local celebrity, and looking at her it wasn't hard for Bolan to see why. She was almost as tall as the soldier, and that was without heels, for her elegant golden thonged sandals were flat. She was wearing a simple sheath dress that clung to her contours, showing her to be finely muscled and well toned. Her hair was styled elegantly, and her jewelery was expensive without being ostentatious. A few simple gold rings, set with small diamonds, and a necklace in tribal design but made from platinum.

She took the lead as they approached the ramp onto the yacht, striding a pace ahead of Bolan. He let her take that lead. She was the one with the invitation. And if the attention was focused on her, the security may not notice that he was the man whose description had been circulated. They expected him to be alone.

"Countess," the security guard said respectfully, with an inclination of his head, as he took the invitation and stepped back to allow her on board. Bolan noted that the other guard was giving the soldier a quizzical look, but when his partner gave him a nod of acknowledgment, the man cast his eyes toward the countess, then smiled in a knowing manner.

Bolan returned the smile, thankful that this obstacle had been passed by a lucky chance, and followed D'Orsini onto the yacht.

On board, the deck space of the spacious vessel was packed with people in various states of intoxication, and Bolan and the countess had to push their way through the throng.

"I must find Hector and thank him for the invitation before we do anything else, darling," she said to Bolan. "A good guest is always polite to the host, and don't you think that he's such a darling host?" she asked, flinging out her arm to indicate the revels around them.

Bolan knew how the host financed his parties, and all he could see were the high-class whores that moved among the guests, the armed security, and the waiters and waitresses who were being importuned, sexually assaulted and insulted by the guests, and all for less than minimum wage, he was sure.

"Yeah, I guess he sure knows how to throw a party," Bolan replied, keeping his voice neutral. At least she was taking him straight to his target. It occurred to him as they made their way toward the prow that the com link between himself and Grimaldi was still open, and the pilot was probably kicking back and thoroughly enjoying what was happening.

The deck area in front of the cabin section had been cleared as a dance floor, and there were catering tables by the cabin walls that were being regularly replenished with alcohol, food and cocaine. There was something for everyone, and a DJ in an old-fashioned booth was spinning the earsplitting disco that was filling the night air of the harbor. As the crowds became more of a crush around the bar, food and drugs, the countess reached back and took Bolan's hand. Her grip was firm, warm and dry. There was something about it that made Bolan wonder if she was all that she seemed.

The crowds thinned as they crossed the dance-floor area, the revelers partying there making their own space with their gyrations. D'Orsini and Bolan threaded their way through, her hand still grasping his.

It was as they passed the booth that Bolan caught sight of Hector Chavez-Smith. He was in conversation with another man the soldier recognized: Mehmet Attaturk, the security adviser to the principality of Saudi Wabu, a small, oil-rich territory that was feeling the squeeze of being between the warring Iran and Iraq, and the richer territories of the OPEC nations, with whom its hard-line Muslim leader had an uneasy alliance. Attaturk was a cold man responsible for many war crimes in Serbia, and the sheikh of Saudi Wabu's insistence on employing him as adviser hadn't exactly helped his relations with the other OPEC nations, who sought to at least maintain an illusion of decency.

More importantly, if Attaturk was there, then it could only mean one thing—negotiations were taking place for the stolen weapons.

The countess walked up to the men, ignoring the cluster of four bodyguards that surrounded them. Chavez-Smith's guards were recognizable as comrades of the others on the boat, but Attaturk had a couple of Slavic guards with eyes as cold as his, and facial scars that spoke of hard combat action. They were leaner, less muscle-bound, but seemed much more likely to retaliate at the first sign of trouble. Even as D'Orsini and Bolan approached, both men stiffened, ready to attack.

"Down, boys," she murmured in a voice that Bolan could

just about hear above the noise. Then, as they neared the arms dealer, she said in louder tones, "Hector, my sweet, so nice of you to invite me to your exclusive little soiree. And my, what interesting company you keep. Who is this divine little man?"

Bolan was perplexed by her behaviour. There was an undertone to her words, a subtext that suggested she had a hidden agenda. But what could it be? He was sure from the way she'd asked that she already knew Attaturk's identity. So was the manner in which she had picked him up anything other than accidental? Bolan smiled and shook hands as he was introduced by the countess to both men. He could feel the disinterest of the bodyguards as they marked her down as a social butterfly, and himself as a gigolo, which would suit him fine. Some small talk was exchanged, but it was obvious that the arms dealer and the military adviser had matters they were impatient to discuss, and D'Orsini soon led Bolan away.

The soldier kept one eye on the small group as he was led to the drinks table. A flute of champagne was thrust into his hand, and he heard the countess whisper, "Lighten up, and don't be so obvious."

It was all he could do not to stare at her in amazement, not because he hadn't figured out she was something other than she pretended, but because he was surprised that she would be so open so soon.

She put her elegant arm around his neck and drew him to her. She kissed him gently on the lips, then put her mouth to his ear.

"Follow my lead," she whispered. Then, louder as she pulled away, "Matt! You naughty, naughty boy. I can't do that in full view of everyone, can I? That will have to wait for later.

But meanwhile…" She giggled and began to walk him toward one of the doors leading into the cabin section.

The manner in which she spoke and acted left little doubt in the minds of those around as to what had occurred, and even the nearby security seemed to be grinning amiably as she pulled at Bolan's arm. She slipped into an open portal and pulled the soldier after her. Once they were out of sight, her manner changed.

"Okay, Matt, we need to find somewhere quiet. We've got some talking to do."

"Both of us," Bolan emphasized.

She nodded and began to lead him down the corridor. "Luckily, I've been here before, and I think I know… Whoa!"

Bolan knew before she had even exclaimed that there was a security patrol coming the other way. He grabbed her and pulled her to him, kissing her hard and running his hands down her body as the security guard rounded the corner of the corridor and caught sight of them.

"Sorry," he said as he passed them, seemingly recognizing the rear view of the countess.

Once he had passed, Bolan tried to disengage from her grasp but found that she was no longer pretending. It was considerably longer than necessary before they broke the embrace, and she gave him a wry smile, her chocolate eyes glistening.

"Well, Matt Cooper, what's your story?"

"So neither of us are what we seem."

She shook her head. "No, and we need to find out if we're on separate missions or if we're going to get in each other's way. I know something big's going down, as all of a sudden we're overrun with operatives."

Bolan frowned. "Overrun?"

She nodded. "Yes, but we need to get some privacy before we discuss this. Come on."

She led the soldier down the corridor and opened the door to a stateroom. Flicking on the light, he could see that it was a bedroom complete with a built-in shower room. The countess led him into the shower.

D'Orsini left the light off and slipped out of her dress. She was naked underneath, and her body was magnificent, even in the darkness of the unlit room. She leaned into the shower and turned on the spray, then moved over to Bolan.

"We took too much of a risk saying as much as we did out there," she said softly. "Hector's a sly old dog, and there are no tricks left to teach him. The whole yacht is bugged, and there are cameras everywhere, except the showers. And once we're under the running water, then we can talk safely."

She extended one of her lithe legs with extreme grace and pushed the shower-room door closed with a flick of her toe.

In the darkness, Bolan quickly shed his outer clothes and the blacksuit, while the countess barred the door as best as possible. After Bolan was naked, they slipped under the running water.

"Now, then, why don't you tell me what exactly a U.S. military man is doing with Hector. I take it I'm correct, and that is a military blacksuit, right?"

"Right enough," Bolan answered.

"Okay, let's try again," she said after a pause. She had expected Bolan to elaborate, but he was giving nothing away. "I'd say your appearance has something to do with that hijacked tanker and whatever went missing. I say this because you're not the only mystery man to suddenly pop up."

"I'm not?"

"No, but I'll trade you that for your confirmation."

"Okay. I'll tell you that you've made a lot of good guesses about me, but you've neglected to fill me in on yourself, Countess."

"Me, sweetheart? I'm a mere nothing."

"I find that hard to believe."

"Flattery might just get you a few answers. I'm part of a team that's here not to monitor Hector so much as to keep an eye on Attaturk."

"Then we may have a conflict of interest. Your target wants to buy the stolen goods I have to recover, and they are probably on board right now."

She shook her head. "The yacht's clean."

"The goods I'm referring to are small in size, about the size of, say, two volumes of an encyclopedia. That's all."

"No, not even that. We have someone on staff—totally reliable—checking it out for us. There's nothing here. If Hector has these goods—"

"We're certain."

"—then they're elsewhere. Also, there are two agents new in town, freelance and dangerous. Real loose cannons, and we haven't managed to figure out who they're working for."

"Would I know them?"

"Maybe. White guy called Jimmy Goldman, and a black guy with the most gorgeous English accent called Errol Ross. Ex-policemen gone bad, then good. Hard, and nasty with it. They're not with the Brits, though, as both MI-5 and -6 hate them. So they're mercs. And they've been sniffing around for something stolen recently."

"Ah, well, I thrive on competition. So it looks like we don't have a conflict of interest after all. I want Chavez-Smith, the stolen goods, and Destiny's Spear. And you—"

"I want to nail Attaturk," D'Orsini finished for him.

"So we can go our own ways, and I know I'm going to have to watch my back for these two guys. In which case, I need to get away from here as soon as possible."

"Maybe that's not as soon as you think." She giggled as she reached for him. "I've got some unfinished business with you."

"We've both got work to do," he murmured, disentangling himself from her. With the shower still running to neutralize any mikes in the bathroom, they dried off and dressed quickly.

"Where was the last place these two rogue agents were seen?" he asked as he slipped back into the blacksuit. "If they've got a head start, I may as well try to catch up and follow, miss the places they've already drawn a blank."

"The last report was earlier this evening, before I came here. They were headed for that dingy little dive with the sewing machines. You know it?"

"I drove past it on the way here," Bolan said ruefully. "I doubt if they'll be there now, but at least I can pick up the trail." He pulled on the pants and shirt that covered the blacksuit. The countess was already dressed, by virtue of having fewer clothes. She looked him up and down appreciatively.

"Maybe our paths will cross again, Matt," she stated. "You ready?"

Bolan nodded, and the countess cleared and opened the shower-room door as Bolan cut the water.

"Darling, that was exquisite," she husked, taking his hand and pulling him into the bedroom, going into her cover act with practiced ease.

They left the bedroom and headed toward the crowded deck. She led the way until they were near the boarding point, when she switched, pretending she was trying to stop him from leaving.

"Are you sure? Are you sure I can't tempt you to stay a little longer?" she implored in what, under other circumstances, he would have been convinced was a genuine manner.

"No, baby, I turn into a pumpkin unless I get home early," he said. "But maybe we can get together later." With which he pulled her to him. "I'll take it from here," he whispered as he held her close, noticing the guards on the board eyeing him in a way that suggested he was a fool to leave her behind. "Good luck with your task."

"And you with yours," she replied softly. Then, louder, "Oh, sweet, do remember where I am."

"I'm not likely to forget," he replied with a smile that gave a clue to his real meaning, as he walked down the ramp and onto the boardwalk and jetty.

He took his last look at D'Orsini, and was sure there was a twinkle and hidden smile. Then she was gone, back to her mission.

And he had some business of his own.

4

Bolan left his car where it was, walking past it on his way back into the city proper. To negotiate the traffic and then try to find another parking space in the crowded streets around the club would waste valuable time. He could walk it in less than ten minutes.

In one way, his brief look at Hector Chavez-Smith had been unproductive. But there were two things he now knew for certain. First, Attaturk was the potential buyer for the stolen weapons, which meant that they had to be near. Second, that wherever they were, the yacht wasn't their location.

"Jack, have you been getting all this," Bolan whispered as he brushed through the crowds coming down the hill toward the harbor.

"Oh yeah…all of it," Grimaldi replied, unable to keep the sly humor out of his voice.

"Okay, so you're up to speed on everything," Bolan answered. "Can you get me some intel on those two guys the countess told me about?"

"Already on it, Sarge," Grimaldi returned, his voice suddenly adopting a more businesslike manner. "The Bear's trying to find out what they're up to, and get some background so you're better informed."

"Good work. I've got a nasty feeling about them. It wouldn't surprise me if they're our guys, but not our guys, if you know what I mean."

"Yeah, I get your drift. What's the plan?"

"Right now, there isn't one," Bolan said. "I can't formulate something until I get a look into that club. Maybe they'll be there, maybe some of the other targets will be there."

"Okay, but keep me up to speed. I'm ready for backup or evac whenever."

"Yeah, I know. And let me have that intel as soon as possible."

"Will do," Grimaldi replied, signing off.

Bolan was now in the square he had earlier driven across, which marked the delineation between the millionaires' row of the yacht harbor, and the poorer area where crime was king. He had been aware of a few people giving him odd stares as he walked past them, muttering, but these days, with hand-free cell phones, it was becoming less and less of a spectacle, and he felt free from observation doing it in an area where the rich would have such toys.

Rarer, though, in the poorer areas, so he was glad that the mike in the blacksuit was concealed, and the earpiece he wore was too much of a miniature to be detected, except by the trained eye. The last thing he wanted now was to draw attention to himself.

He walked across the square and down into the maze of cobbled streets housing bars and clubs. These streets had a different atmosphere. The people were not on show. They were living their lives moment by moment, and all they wanted was a good night out. Without the level of scrutiny that he had along the harbor, it was easier for the soldier to study the crowds without being eyed suspiciously.

The third cobbled street along, Rue Madelaine, housed the Club Noir. Black, as simple and easily identifiable as that. How the sewing machines came into the equation, apart from the fact that it once been a factory, he couldn't fathom. But that was unimportant. What mattered was that it was one of the best-known clubs in Marseilles, and it was the one mentioned by the countess.

Bolan walked down the street, keeping to the center, where the crowds were less congested. Only strangers drove down these roads by night, so traffic was sparse, and it was easy for him to move out of the way of any oncoming vehicles. The wallet in his pocket contained more than enough currency for the evening ahead—he knew how extortionate French club prices could be from previous visits.

A piercing wolf whistle to his left drew his attention.

Bolan turned and saw two women sitting on the step of a tenement. One was in her late twenties, with dyed black hair cropped short. She wore an orange halter top and faded blue jeans. The other was perhaps a couple of years younger, and had curls in varying shades of blond that tumbled over her shoulders, spilling onto the thigh-length print dress she wore. From the way in which the black-haired girl was laughing and prodding the other, it was the blonde who had whistled.

"Yeah, I'm talking to you, mister," she said in heavily accented English. "I saw you drive through earlier. What happened? Someone steal your car?"

"I decided to leave it back along the way," Bolan said easily, gesturing behind him, "maybe catch some nightlife."

"Yeah, you'll get plenty of that along here, then go back

to find your car gone. Everything gets stolen around here. You a tourist?"

Bolan gestured. "Not really, just passing through."

"And want a little fun?"

"Could be." If the girls were whores, it was one of the most obtuse approaches he'd ever come across. The blonde obviously read his hesitation.

"Hey, this is not a business deal. I whistled at you because I like the look of you. But I tell you something…"

"What?"

"You want to take me out, then you have to pay. I'm just a poor girl."

Bolan walked over to the step, hunkering down in front of her. "And where would you want to go? I was thinking of checking out that club over there," he added, indicating the Club Noir.

"Oh, you wouldn't want to go there. Very dangerous for someone just passing through," she said mockingly.

"So I'd need a guide, someone who knows the area, knows the clubs."

"I'd offer to help, after all, you're a nice looking guy, but you know how it is."

"Your friend comes too, or is it just you?"

"Oh no, just me." She smiled, bounding to her feet and taking his arm as he straightened. "Let me tell you something, you won't forget this in a hurry," she said, hugging close to him. Then, over her shoulder, "See ya, Claudette."

Bolan strolled back across the street, the girl clinging to him. Getting into the club with the girl as cover would make him much less suspicious. But on the downside, she was someone to look out for if a firefight broke out, which was always a possibility if he caught up with the freelance agents, especially if they were as wild as D'Orsini suggested.

"So what's your name?"

"Mickey to you. But Michelle if you're French."

"I'm Matt."

She pulled away from him. "Hey, Matt, you do have the francs to get in, right?"

"Oh yeah," he said as they joined the throng around the entrance to the club. From inside he could hear the pounding of drums and screaming guitars. It was more of a punk and metal club than a dance venue, which made a change—pleasant or not he didn't like to say—from Chavez-Smith's party.

Immediately, he saw the advantage in having the girl with him as she pushed her way through the throng, dragging him with her as she cursed at those around them. They came up in front of the old, wooden double doors, most likely the same ones that were in place when the club had been a factory, and were faced with two doormen who looked far more solid than the doors themselves. Both were huge black men who stood more than six and a half feet tall, with their impassive stares hidden behind wraparound shades. One had dreadlocks, and the other had a shaved head. That was the only thing that set them apart, as they both obviously spent a lot of time in the gym. In cutoff T-shirts and tight black jeans, with black sneakers, their clothes were chosen to emphasize their muscular frames.

And yet both of them cracked wide grins as the blonde approached.

"Hey, 'Chelle, you been away long time, now," Dreadlocks said with a thick dockside Marseilles accent.

The girl shrugged. "Yeah. Sometimes I need a change. So you going to let me in? And my friend Matt, of course."

"Of course we are," Dreadlocks said, standing aside and then bending to offer his cheek as the blonde stood on tiptoe to kiss him chastely. She led Bolan through the doors, and as he passed Dreadlocks, the man whispered, "'Chelle a good girl. You look after her or else."

This was promising. Bolan had a guide to the club who knew the staff—and probably the regular clientele—very well. Hopefully, Goldman and Ross didn't have the same advantage.

Of course, there was always the chance that this was a setup. Security was never one hundred percent, no matter who one was, or what organization one worked for. He had been spotted on the yacht, and perhaps not just by the countess. The soldier had a nose for trouble, and the girl seemed fine, but caution had kept him alive this far, so he would roll with it.

They headed for the bar, the crush of people making the club seem claustrophobic. The club was black in every way: the walls, ceiling and floor were painted that color, and there was little, if any, air-conditioning. The low-level lighting barely illuminated more than a couple of feet in front of them as they moved toward the bar. It was only around the bar and stage, where light reflected from those areas, that the visibility was better.

The layout of the club suggested that it was rectangular, extending back some way in length, while the width was narrow. Which made the positioning of tables and chairs all the more ridiculous. In theory, it had to have had a small capacity, but the crowd of people suggested that this was being judiciously ignored.

The bar occupied the right-hand wall near the entrance, with three bar staff coping with the crush of customers pressing against the counter. Beyond, at the back of the room and down a three-step drop, the stage was recessed, suggesting that the club did widen out a little. This was lit by a battery of colored lights, and was occupied by a five-piece band, the drummer hidden by his kit and banks of amplifiers. The two guitarists, bassist and vocalist were in full view. Those with long hair flailed it around in wet stands, while the bass player's bald head was spangled with sweat that glistened in the lights. T-shirts were soaked, and the singer's bare chest was streaked not just with sweat, but from blood that streamed from his nose. The wild mosh pit dancers in front of the stage suggested how this injury had occurred. Even by small club standards, the band was incredibly loud, and Bolan wondered how he could effectively communicate with the girl, let alone hear any intel that Grimaldi would send.

The girl had fought her way through to the front of the bar, Bolan behind her, and had caught the eye of bartender who was obviously pleased to see her. He ignored the customers in front of him and came over to her. She ordered herself a beer and caught Bolan's eye. He nodded and handed over the money, then took the bottle, which dripped ice-cold condensation from the cooler.

"Come on," the girl mouthed, leading him past the stage area, skirting the pit, and toward the rear of the club. At the back, hidden from view by the stage was a soundproofed door guarded by another large black security man. Despite the darkness inside the club, he, too, was wearing wraparound shades.

"Hey, Charlie," the blonde yelled at him, "let us in?"

A large grin broke his face, although the eyes were still impassive behind the shades. He opened the door as they neared, and the blonde took Bolan through into a long, narrow room. As the soundproofed door closed behind them, the roar of the band was cut to a muffled thud, and the conversation in the back room became a louder hum.

"This is better. At least you can hear yourself think," Bolan said wryly.

"Yeah, I didn't have you figured for a headbanger. And there's no way you would have known about this room without me, is there?" she added coquettishly. "So maybe you should be nice to me."

"Yeah, why not," the soldier agreed.

She led him to a table and draped herself over him.

"I know what you think I am, but I'm not. I just like the look of a guy, then I go for it. I figure, if guys can do it, why can't I? And I like the look of you a lot." Her voice had slipped from little girl into predator, making Bolan suppress a smile. She continued, in the same tone, "So why don't you tell me a little about yourself, Matt?"

Bolan began to talk. She hung on his every word, with a sexual hunger in her eyes. He gave her a cover story about being a U.S. journalist doing a feature on the south of France for a possible travel book. He'd spent so many years undercover in one form or another, having to keep his true identity and history secret, that it was incredibly easy to tell these lies.

It seemed to the girl as though he were pouring out his heart to her, sometimes telling her something that cut so deep that he had to look away. In fact, although in one sense he hated the deceit, he had become so used to covering his tracks that he was able to be consistent with his lies without even thinking about it, and he used the emotional moments where he had to look away to survey the rest of the back room.

It was obvious that this was a private section, for use only by a select clientele. At first glance, he was sure that he could see money changing hands for drugs and information, and there were some seamen looking as though a hijacking on the docks wouldn't come as a surprise to them. Whores and pimps argued with clients, and even though it was obviously an openly criminal place, there were proprieties to be observed, as he saw money change hands over the table, but automatic pistols and revolvers wrapped in oilcloth were passed under the table.

The room itself was about twenty feet deep, with a small bar in one corner. It was a drinking den rather than anything else, and the lighting was dim but sufficient. He had little trouble surveying the room.

"Anyway, I know nothing about you," Bolan said suddenly. "Let me get you another beer, and then you can tell me about yourself."

"That'd be cool." She smiled at him as he got up and went over to the bar which enabled him to get a full view of the whole room. And what he saw gave him pause for thought.

Bolan paid for the drinks and returned to the table.

"Thanks," she said, clinking bottles with him. "So you want to know about me? Well, I'll tell you…"

The girl launched into a story. She was orphaned in her early teens, and rather than go into a state home she had run away and started living on the streets. That was where she had met Claudette, another runaway. They had worked menial jobs, and scrimped and saved to rent a small garret near the club. She had never become a whore, despite the efforts of local pimps. She and Claudette had been street girls, and knew nearly everyone in the quarter.

It sounded a little too much like a French film to be entirely true, and Bolan was sure he was getting a version that was either cleaned up for him, or was the idealized version that she dearly wished that she had lived. As she talked, Bolan surveyed the room.

Sitting in the corner with a woman was Salvatore Signella.

Two tables away were a redheaded guy and an elegantly dressed black man. The white guy was talking animatedly, his partner replying sparingly. Bolan caught enough of the dialogue to realize that they were speaking English.

Ross and Goldman.

5

"Mickey," Bolan said softly but with insistence, breaking across her rambling tale and making her stop dead with the quiet force of his tone. It was just the one word, but enough.

"Why do I get the feeling there is going to be trouble," she asked in a plaintive tone.

The soldier had to smile. "Sorry, but it's not my fault. I've just got this feeling, too. Without being obvious about it, can you tell me if you know anything about the Sicilian in the corner, and the two guys arguing a couple of tables away?"

The girl raised her beer bottle, using the motion to take a look toward the end of the room. She took a long draft, eyeing the men Bolan had indicated. When she put the bottle on the table she leaned across and grasped his hand, looking into his eyes as though they were getting more intimate.

She was a good actress, Bolan had to give her that.

"The two English who are arguing I've never seen before. I only know they are English because I can hear them. But if they're connected with the other guy, then it's trouble all right."

"You know him, then." It was a statement, not a question.

"Not that well, but still more than I wished I did. Salvo, they call him. I don't want to know any more than that. The slut with him is Celeste. She works the dock area. I guess that's where he gets his information from."

Bolan grasped her hand. "You know what he's involved in?"

The girl gave a brief shake of her head. "Only that he's a hard man—even Charlie is scared of him," she added, indicating the security man on the other side of the door. "Salvo is frightened of nothing and doesn't think about getting hurt. He used to work security down at the harbor for some rich guy, but next thing he's hanging about with petty thieves and political idealists," she spit. "He's into stealing and violence. I think a lot of crime around here is his fault, but I keep well away."

"I can't say that I blame you," Bolan said softly. "Now listen. I wasn't exactly truthful with you, but I know I can trust you well enough, and I don't want you to get hurt. Some of what I said was true, but the fact is that I'm in Marseilles to try to track down the man you call Salvo. The other two guys are also after him. In a room like this, with the four people involved, it's going to get tough. And I don't want you involved in that. So I want you to go. Walk out of that door, walk out of the club and don't come back for a very long time. Because people like Charlie and the other guys on the door may wonder about me, and about how involved you are. Will you do that for me?"

Michelle reached up and cradled his cheek in her hand. "I appreciate what you're doing for me."

The girl stood and walked toward the door without looking back. Bolan sat watching her, waiting until she had pulled open the soundproofed door, briefly letting in a burst of heavy-metal thunder before it closed on the room. He counted ten, but the door didn't open again, with an angry Charlie headed for him. There was always a chance that she would have gone straight to the security and told them what was going down. But she didn't.

Bolan turned toward the rear of the room, rising from his seat. He scanned the room, taking in the two mercenaries, drinking now in silence. The black man—Ross—gave him a brief look. His brow furrowed, as though an instinct had given him a sniff of trouble ahead.

Move fast.

Bolan slipped a button on the loose shirt and reached under to where the Desert Eagle was holstered. He ignored the two mercs and concentrated for the next few moments on his target. Signella was pawing at the woman Celeste, his hand in her blouse. His other hand was out of sight.

Bolan slipped onto the seat opposite Signella. The Sicilian, catching the soldier entering his field of vision, grunted in surprise and tore his attention away from the woman.

"Fuck off, this is a private table, not a floor show," he said with a sneer, his French heavily accented with his native Italian.

"It is, but she's not the attraction. You are," Bolan said quietly, the menace in his tone belying the smile he adopted for any onlookers.

Through his drunken haze, Signella frowned, realizing something was wrong but not able to pinpoint what it was.

Bolan drew the Desert Eagle quickly and aimed it under the table, where it was trained on the man's crotch. The move was smooth enough to be almost hidden from those around, but showed enough of the hardware to the Sicilian to signal intent.

"You won't be much good to her without balls, so listen very carefully," Bolan said quietly.

"Who the fuck are you?"

"Doesn't matter. All you need to remember is that I'm the one with the gun," Bolan said calmly. "We've got a lot to talk about, and it won't be here."

"Look, I'm surrounded by friends in here. You try anything and—"

"Not all are friends," Bolan interrupted. "If you look two tables down, you'll see a white guy with red hair and a black guy. They're looking at us now and I tell you, they're not friends. Yours or mine. And they want you, too. I'm giving you the option to cooperate. They won't. If it was them sitting here, you would have already been killed."

He paused, waiting a beat to see how Signella reacted.

The Sicilian didn't let him down.

"Okay, we talk. But when I see you again after this, I'll kill you very slowly."

"I think that's a risk I'm prepared to take," Bolan replied. "Now get up and move toward the door, slowly. I'll be behind you, and I'll have the gun on you the whole time."

"How are you going to manage that?" Signella asked, as he adopted the puzzled tone of a fellow professional faced with a problem.

Bolan grinned. "Let me worry about that. You just do as I say. And as for you—" he turned his attention to the woman "—give me your shawl."

The puzzled woman gave Bolan the heavy shawl that was hanging off one shoulder.

"Yeah, I'll take it. Thanks," he said in a voice loud enough to be heard at the next table. Still holding it in his free hand, he brought out the Desert Eagle and draped it over his arm and hand, as though stretching it out to examine it. "Yeah, it looks really good," he said in the same voice, before dropping the level to add, "I'm going to be looking at this as I follow you out. It's heavy enough to get entangled after one shot, but that's all I need. Remember that."

Signella nodded. "Not bad," he said, indicating the shawl. "I'll remember that. Maybe use it when I kill you."

"You've got to get out of here first. Now move."

Signella stood and motioned for the whore to stay behind as she made to join him. Bolan rose with him, allowing Signella to move out from behind the table, and standing well back so that the Sicilian couldn't simply flip it over at him.

As Signella moved down the room to the far door, he glanced nervously over his shoulder to see where Bolan was. If there was any opportunity of taking him, he suddenly found his path blocked by the two mercenaries as they rose from their table.

It was a standoff, but in the dim light and the general activity of the back-room bar, it wasn't obvious to any but those taking part.

"Hang on, you're being a bit presumptuous, aren't you?" the redheaded man—Goldman—said with a nervous twitch.

"What my friend means is, why do you have to leave so soon?"

Signella scowled. He had two men in front of him, and a gun at his back. Bolan knew he couldn't fight back. The only option was to set three men at one another's throats while he made a getaway. Bolan would avoid that if possible.

"Hey, who do you work for?" Bolan called to them, his voice cutting through the background noise.

Goldman frowned heavily and quickly glanced at Ross, who remained impassive.

"I hear you two are CIA. Maybe gendarmes?" The soldier switched to French as he said the second sentence, knowing what effect it would have.

"Oh, for fuck's sakes, did you have to do that?" Ross

sighed heavily, reaching into his immaculately pressed jacket and pulling out a 9 mm Beretta that matched the one Bolan had stowed in his blacksuit.

The sight of the Beretta in full view caused an immediate change in the room. A tense silence had descended when the word gendarmes had cut through the noise, and the clientele near the back bar had been waiting to see what would develop.

Above all else, Bolan wanted Signella alive. And he knew that the two freelancers wanted that as well. But would circumstances allow them to accomplish that and get out? The atmosphere had changed to one of hostility, and it was directed solely at the two mercs, Bolan being seen by the crowd as with Signella rather than against him.

Ross's finger tightened on the trigger of the Beretta, and he began to arc the weapon around, firing indiscriminately into the crowds at the tables. Bolan dived for cover and pushed Signella so that the Sicilian stumbled and fell, the arc of fire just missing him as he sprawled across a table.

From his position on the floor, Bolan suddenly realized that this was not the random act that it had at first appeared. As Ross continued to fire, Goldman drew a snub-nosed .38-caliber Smith & Wesson revolver and grabbed for Signella, hauling him to his feet and holding the gun to his head. He barked a few words that Bolan couldn't hear above the roar of gunfire in the enclosed space, and Signella nodded quickly.

Some of the customers were dead or injured, the 9 mm rounds ripping into them at close range. But most had either been out of range or were simply too quick. They were under cover before Ross could complete his circuit of fire. Those who were armed had already drawn their weapons.

Ross was still firing, backing away toward the door.

Some of the customers had begun to fire back, but the impeccably dressed black agent was impassive, ignoring the bullets that riddled the wall and bar around him. He had an almost fatalistic air. If he was going to be hit, then it would happen anyway, and there was nothing he could do to stop it. He would trust fate. That worked for him. It made him seem formidable to those who were firing at him, although most of this was blind fire, so it increased his odds.

What concerned Bolan more was the activity of Goldman and Signella to the rear of Ross. The Sicilian was up on his feet, starting to tug at the door, Goldman at his back with the Smith & Wesson firmly in his ribs. They would have the door open and be out into the main area of the club—and the cover of darkness—before the soldier could be on his feet to go after them. He was pinned down both by Ross's covering fire, and the random shooting of the other club patrons.

Signella tugged the door open, and the sound of gunfire had to have cut over the sound of the band, as Charlie turned his head.

Bolan saw him reaching for the mike on his headset, which would connect him to the rest of the security in the club. They were the last words he would ever utter, as Goldman stepped out from behind Signella and shot him in the face at point-blank range. The redheaded merc was covered with blood, brain, and slivers of flesh and bone as the .38-caliber round took off the back of the security man's head, and obliterated his astonished expression.

As the guard fell back, and the sounds of the metal band pounded around the small back room, cutting out the noises of the gunfire, Goldman and Signella moved into the darkness of the club, Ross backing out after them, still firing. He used his free hand to swing the door closed behind him.

A last, stray shot cracked against the door as it shut with a soft thud, leaving the back bar stinking of cordite. The stunned patrons, some still holding their guns, looked around. Who was to blame for what had happened? Should they risk opening the door and being framed perfectly in the light from the bar, against the dark of the club beyond?

Bolan sprang to his feet, losing the shawl as he did and exposing the Desert Eagle in his fist. He had to take the chance. He couldn't afford to lose Signella and the two free-lancers. With them, the trail to the chemical weapons and the sonic weapons died. Besides which, they had pulled civilians into what was supposed to be a private battle. These people were probably criminals for the most part, albeit petty in the bigger picture, but that didn't give anyone the right to kill them indiscriminately.

And there was one other thing—if he didn't get out of there soon, then Celeste would point the finger at him, and he would have to kill a few people to get out alive.

Bolan was at the door in a few strides before anyone else in the room had time to gather their wits.

"Jack, are you still on-line?" he yelled.

"Affirmative, Sarge," Grimaldi's voice said in his earpiece. "What's been going on?"

"Ross and Goldman have Signella, and they've put me into the middle of a bear pit. Any intel on them yet?"

"Negative. Aaron tells me that there's some heavy-duty blocking going on. Whoever these guys are working for doesn't want anything known about them."

"Great, just great. Keep me monitored."

"Affirmative. I'd say good luck, but you don't need that."

"I think I always need it, Jack," Bolan commented as he crouched and pulled the door open from his lowered position. It took immense strength to pull the heavily insulated door open because of the angle of leverage, but Bolan had developed and strengthened muscles that had been trained and honed for such tasks. As the door began to swing, he threw himself through the gap, just clearing Charlie's body, and rolling to come up on his feet out of the line of the light from the back bar.

The band was grinding to a halt, only the bass player still thrashing at his instrument, as they gradually became aware of the altercation. The mosh pit had emptied, and an ever-widening space was growing around the stage as Ross, Goldman and Signella moved across the floor. The spray of fire that Ross sent at the open door as Bolan dived out was the final nail in the band's coffin. With just the bass now filling the room, the staccato sound of the exploding Beretta cut through the darkened room, spreading fear and panic to those clubbers who had not, as yet, realized that something was wrong.

At the sound of this final blast, pandemonium cut loose. The bassist stopped playing, dropped his instrument as he struggled out of the strap and dived for the back of the stage. His fellow band members had already leaped for cover. Those clubbers who were trapped between the gunman and the entrance huddled against the back wall, opposite the stage. Those up in the bar area near the entrance were trying desperately to get out through the double doors, falling over one another in panic. Against their tide, the bouncers from the door were trying to fight their way in, to see what was happening. They yelled into their headsets, wondering where their opposite numbers were within the club.

Which was exactly what Bolan was wondering as the mercenaries cut a swath toward the exit. He also wondered how they planned to get past the gridlock that was the sole exit.

Errol Ross ejected the empty clip from the Beretta, reached smoothly and swiftly into his pocket, then rammed home a full clip. The action was quick and efficient, practiced without his even looking. His attention was focused on the darkened interior of the club. There was a little illumination from the stage, and a further source from the open door of the back room. He was able to see that the clubbers left in the dance area were huddled against the wall, trying to stay clear of his covering fire.

Among them was the man who had tried to take Signella.

Dammit, who the hell was he? Ross wondered. His eyes narrowed as he tried to pierce the gloom by sheer force of will. The way the man had spoken to them suggested that he was after Signella for the same thing. So what branch of intelligence or the Justice Department did he work for? Was he even working for the U.S.? If they were freelancing, then so, too, could he. It was even possible that they had both been hired by the same department. These people were so good at keeping things hidden, laying down smoke screens, that it was entirely possible that they would set two lots of operatives at each other's throats to try to increase the competition, get the job done faster.

No wonder they were all so damned paranoid.

So paranoid that he was sure he could see the man moving in the shadows, getting closer.

BOLAN USED THE COVER of the darkness to move forward. He kept low, the Desert Eagle in one hand, the other probing in front of him. He kept whispering "Keep calm, don't worry, let me through" in French as he moved. He doubted that the terrified clubbers could make out what he was saying, much less understand, but he was desperate to avoid a situation where some panicked and opened up the way for a massacre. He could see the shape of Ross, standing at the foot of the shallow stairs leading up to the bar area, the main site of congestion. But the man's face was in darkness. Bolan watched him eject the clip and replace it. One clear shot could have taken out the merc at this point, but Bolan wanted both Ross and Goldman alive. Taking out one may panic the other into killing Signella.

"JIMMY, WHAT'S GOING ON up there?" Ross yelled over his shoulder.

"Gridlock." Goldman returned with the anger boiling over into his voice. "And don't you try anything or else I'll kill you," he added in a quieter voice to Signella.

The unarmed Sicilian could see the gleam in Goldman's eye that told him the redhead meant business. It also told him this would be a stupid place for him to die.

"Do something," Ross screamed.

The whole thing had gone wrong. Their intention had been to wait while Signella got drunk with his whore, follow them out of the club, then take him. They could spirit him away for questioning, then recover the target and get out. It was simple.

But this? Stuck in a darkened club with another agent firing at them, unable to get out of the place because of the crush of people, and liable to lose Signella either to a bullet or the crowds. Why the hell had this other guy turned up now? Ross wondered. They'd had no choice but to step in. They couldn't let Signella be taken from under their noses.

"Jimmy, just shoot your way out," Ross shouted.

"If I could, I would," Goldman returned. "But I'd need an M-60 to cut through this."

"WHAT'S HAPPENING, man?" the dreadlocked doorman yelled into his headset. From where they were, on the outside of the club, it was almost impossible to hear the gunshots over the throb of the band and the noise from the streets. All he and his partner knew was that suddenly there was a rush from the inside, and people were spilling out, colliding with those who wanted to enter, or were just hanging out in the streets. They had exchanged puzzled glances and asked for information from inside. There were two other security men working the inside, apart from Charlie on the back-room door. Charlie's mike seemed to have gone dead, and in the rush the other security guards were too busy to answer immediately.

And then the band had ceased to play, and the chatter of sporadic gunfire could be heard.

"Shit! We've got to get the doors clear," the bald doorman yelled, his impassive face cracking for the first time that evening.

"How?"

"Kick them back if you have to, so we can get these open," his partner replied, using his muscle to push against the seething, yet jammed, throng of humanity in the doorway.

If the two doormen could actually get into the club, then clearing the jam would be relatively simple. They were guarding two doors built into the larger double doors of the old factory, in much the same way that many nineteenth-century factories and warehouses had large doors for delivery, but smaller doors inset for staff and workers to use. The doors were solid enough, and were secured by massive old iron bolts that slipped into the floor at the bottom, and the stone door lintel at the top. To slip these bolts and open the doors, relieving the crush, was—in theory—the work of seconds.

Not so easy when a mass of panicking customers were pushing their way out.

"Back! Just get back and everything will be fine," the guard yelled in a tone that suggested otherwise, all the while kicking his way into the mass. On the other side, his partner did likewise. He wasn't paid to hurt the clubbers, but he knew that if they couldn't free the gridlock, then people would get crushed, and who knew how many would get killed if the shooting inside continued. He didn't want to think about the gunfire, as he knew that he and the other security men were unarmed.

On each side of the door, now, they had made enough space for themselves to move freely. Each man kicked up the floor bolt, their heavy shoes still not thick enough to stop the iron bolts from jarring the bones in their feet. Pain they could ignore under the circumstances, as adrenaline shot through their veins.

In unison, like a well-oiled machine, they reached up for the bolts jammed into the stone lintel, the scrape of the little-used device making it hard to move the bolts. Both men swore as they maneuvered the metal from side to side, cursing the club owners who wouldn't spare a little oil for these eventualities.

Dreadlocks moved his bolt first, letting it drop and putting his shoulder to the crowd behind him as he tried to pull the door, pushing them backward to make room for the sweep of the massive wooden door. He knew that those directly behind would see what he was doing and be thankful. They weren't the problem. It was those a little farther back who were causing the obstruction, still pushing forward and trying to escape. Sweat poured off him as he pushed back, feeling the heaving mass of people to his rear.

The bald doorman was only a fraction of a second behind him, and although the night air from the Marseilles street beyond was humid and warm, it was still cooler than the rank aura in the club's bar area. The air tasted sweet to those in the front of the crush, who pushed their way through the ever-widening gap.

The doormen got the doors back as far as they would go, and the trickle into the street turned into a flood as clubbers fell over themselves to get out, and away from the shooting. The two security men were prevented from getting farther into the club by the sudden, lemminglike exodus as the flow of traffic pinned them to the walls.

"ERROL, HEADS UP. Something's happening," Goldman yelled as the lights from the street outside became visible from inside the club.

Signella saw Ross look over his shoulder. "What the—"

The gap became wider, and people stared to move. It was at this moment that Goldman looked backward, to try to locate his partner.

Signella—all the earlier alcoholic muzziness driven from his system by fear and the will to survive—noticed that Goldman's attention was momentarily taken away from him. They seemed to want him alive. Would they actually take him out? If he stayed, they certainly would.

Time to play percentages.

Before Goldman had a chance to react, Signella brought up his left elbow so that it connected with the redhead's arm, jerking the Smith & Wesson revolver toward the ceiling. At the same time, he forearm-punched the woman in front of him, making her stumble to one side. The small gap this left was all he needed. Elbows and forearms carving a path through the clubbers in front of him, moving easier as the flow increased and he was able to use its momentum, Signella was lost in the dingy crowd of featureless heads and shoulders before Goldman had a chance to locate him.

BOLAN WAS RELIEVED when the shooting stopped. At least the two mercs didn't want to shoot their way through. No need now that the gridlock was freed, but he never knew with such loose cannons.

He knew that Signella had broken from them, and they were too far in front of Bolan. So the chances of Signella being within his view were pretty slim. The best he could hope for was to follow Ross and Goldman, and hope that they would lead him in the right direction. Always assuming that they didn't want to just blow him away.

Keeping track of them was going to be difficult. The sight of the double doors opening, the crowds beginning to move, and Ross disappearing into the throng had given the huddled clubbers the impetus to make a move of their own, and they, too, were rushing for the exit—with Bolan in the middle of them, trying to keep Ross and Goldman in sight.

Bolan holstered the Desert Eagle, wanting to appear as inconspicuous as possible. It was unlikely that he could be readily identified without hardware in his hand, and he was relying on a fast evac.

The soldier cut his way through the people, keeping his eyes on the figure of Ross as he cut a swath into the now freely flowing crowd. He didn't want to lose sight of him, but that was no problem. The immaculately dressed mercenary stood out because of his designer clothing.

Ross, about twelve yards ahead of Bolan, reached the double doors and disappeared to the left. Anxious not to lose sight of him, Bolan redoubled his efforts to get through the crowd.

"WHERE DID THAT Sicilian go?" Ross asked himself as he came out onto the street, straightening his jacket unconsciously, the Beretta neatly holstered. "And where is that Irish idiot?"

Before deciding to be partners, Ross did his research. He knew all about the twisted lineage of Jimmy Goldman. Although he had a Jewish father, he had an Irish Catholic mother, and had been brought up entirely by her side of the family after his father had absconded with someone else's business profits following the collapse of his accountancy company. The strange mix of cultures often caused the redhead to lose his temper at the slightest provocation. Which was why Ross was anxious to keep close on his tail. He wouldn't put it past Goldman to try to get the information from Signella quickly by kneecapping him in a dark alley.

That wouldn't get them where they wanted to be. Ross was sure of that. He scanned up and down the street, desperately trying to make out a familiar face or body shape in the teeming crowd.

There, down across the square, was Goldman, and he was walking quickly, in hot pursuit of Signella. Ross knew this as he caught sight of the Sicilian disappearing into an alleyway. Chances were that it was a dead end, as the back of the

buildings lining the square on that side came up against ho-
tels marking the beginnings of the rich quarter.

Signella was all theirs.

BOLAN CAME OUT of the club in time to see Ross striding across
the square. Following Signella and Goldman into an alley?

"Jack, do you copy?" Bolan asked as he followed the merc.

"Yeah, I'm with you, Sarge," Grimaldi replied. "Exactly
what the hell happened in there?"

"Goldman and Ross took Signella, then started a firefight
in the club. But the idiots have let him get away. I'm following them right now, hoping that they're actually following
him, but I need some intel, fast."

"I'll do my best," Grimaldi said.

"Have you got any blueprints and plans for Marseilles?
Not just street maps, but something else…maybe with the
sewers, any railways, something like that?"

There was a moment's silence, then Grimaldi broke it,
sounding elated. "That boy Walters is going to go a long
way, Striker, you mark my words."

"I take it that means yes, then," Bolan muttered dryly.

"Oh yeah. What do you need to know, Sarge? I have the
complete blueprints for the city in a nice little folder."

"I hope it has an index. This is a big place," Bolan said. "I'm
in Avignons Square, and I need to know about all the streets on
the south side, leading to the harbor. Have they got dead ends,
and have they got an access to the sewers and tunnels beneath."

While he spoke, he made his way around the square, trying to use the people walking the sidewalks as cover. Although Ross had strode straight across, Bolan was loathe to
do this in case the merc looked back. The last thing the soldier wanted out in the open like this was another firefight.

Especially when it seemed that the freelancers were conveniently leading him into a closed scenario that would make fighting much easier—and less likely to take out innocent bystanders.

It took Grimaldi only a few moments to find the intel Bolan wanted, by which time the soldier had made his way to the entrance of the alley.

"It's called the Rue Vendredi, Jack," he whispered, standing on the left of the alleyway, with his back to the shopfront that cornered the road.

"Got it. It's a dead end, all right, but there's a storm drain cover at the closed end, just before the rear exterior wall of the Hotel Concorde. There's a yard over that wall, about three yards to the rear of the building itself."

"I don't think they'll be going over that wall, somehow," Bolan mused. "I'm going in, Jack. Keep the line open."

A storm drain cover. Marseilles was built on a slope that led toward the harbor and the docks, with the storm drain presumably opening out onto the sea along the harbor and dockside walls. With the sometimes heavy rains coming down from the hills, and the high water table of a chalk soil that edged onto the sea, Bolan was sure that the system had to be extensive—and large enough to accommodate a man.

If the mercs were following Signella this far, then the chances were that he'd used the storm drain as an escape route.

It would be a maze. Easier to lose them, and easier to be heard, as they would be the only ones down there.

ROSS COULDN'T BELIEVE what he was seeing as he quickened his pace down the alley. In front of him, by the wall that cut off any further passage, his partner was disappearing down a manhole.

"Jimmy," Ross whispered.

Point Position

Goldman held up a hand and replied in a similarly subdued tone. "He's down here. So you want to follow him or what? He's the only lead." And before his partner had a chance to argue, the redhead had lowered himself below street level.

Ross looked at his immaculately cut suit and expensive loafers. His socks were silk, and so fine that they were almost transparent. His shirt was the finest linen he could purchase in Saville Row, London.

With a sigh, Errol Ross hurried across to the open manhole and sat beside it, tentatively feeling with his feet for any iron staples or rungs that would act as a foothold or ladder to the drains below. His loafers were so exquisitely made that he could feel every contour of the brickwork surrounding the rungs as his foot made contact. So exquisitely made that they would soon be decimated by the sewers below.

"Oh, shit," Ross muttered as he lowered himself into the manhole and pulled the cover across in his wake.

BOLAN WATCHED Ross disappear, and the manhole cover swing back into place. As it slid smoothly into its groove and fit flush to the surface of the alley, Bolan began to move toward it. He knew that he would have to be careful, as the mercs would be able to hear him clearly in the storm drains unless he exacted extreme caution.

The soldier covered the ground to the iron cover, then knelt with his ear to it. Faintly, he could hear the sounds of movement, growing more and more distant. He counted to ten slowly, then began to inch the cover from the opening. His eyebrow shot up in surprise as the cover lifted easily. It was heavy, but the groove into which it fit had been kept greased and free from rust and dirt. Obviously, it was a commonly used route into the drains.

But why? Who, other than Signella, would use this route?

Bolan, adopting a worst-case scenario to be prepared, could see that an underground storm drain system would provide a viable alternative route around the city for a number of parties that would not wish to be seen above ground—the kind of people who would carry some serious hardware.

He wondered if this had also occurred to Ross and Goldman. If so, it would make them much more wary, and so Bolan would need to proceed with extreme caution, lest they should detect his presence.

"I'm going underground now, Jack," he whispered into the mike in his blacksuit. "I doubt this'll transmit for a while, but keep monitoring."

"You bet," Grimaldi replied briefly, not wishing to waste words or time.

Bolan moved the metal cover to one side of the alley, then lowered his body into the gap, using his arms to support his weight as his feet hung in the air, searching for a foothold. He found the iron rungs and climbed down a little way, until he could grasp the cover and pull it into place over his head.

The darkness seemed sudden and all-engulfing as the cover slotted back into place above his head, lowered with an infinite gentleness to avoid any sound. Even the barest scrape of metal on gravel and concrete made him wince. In the dark and enclosed space of the ladder tunnel it seemed to be exaggeratedly loud. In truth, it was probably inaudible, blocked by the bulk of his body within the narrow channel.

There were twelve rungs in the ladder, which seemed to be spaced about a foot and a half apart, so he figured they had dropped about eighteen feet below the surface. On number thirteen—or what should have been—his foot dangled into air. He looked over his shoulder and found a gap opening beneath him, with a dim illumination that seemed as bright as lighting after the darkness in which he'd descended.

Bolan drew his foot back up to the last rung and stilled his breath, listening intently. Apart from the blood pounding in his ears, he could hear the faint traces of men splashing through the shallows of the storm drain, echoing distantly, to his left, heading toward the openings by the docks, unless he was mistaken.

Two things occurred to him. If Signella was heading that way and the terrorist cell had a base near the docks, then it was a clear case of hiding in plain sight. And if he could hear Ross and Goldman—and possibly Signella—then it was certain that the Sicilian would realize he was being followed.

All of which changed the percentages somewhat. It was now possible that rather than a tracking operation, the soldier would find himself walking into a firefight. And it was also a certain bet that his own presence would be detected as he followed.

Bolan judged the distance between the last rung and the floor of the storm drain and braced himself as he dropped.

He landed with a splash, as there was half an inch of water gathered on the floor of the giant pipe, flowing sluggishly in the direction of his fleeing targets. He stood silently, listening and allowing his eyes to adjust to the light. The storm drains were large concrete pipes, laid in the last twenty to thirty years and coated with a reflective, luminous paint that enabled them to trap and enhance the light that filtered through at several points from roadside inlets. They were about eight feet in circumference, giving a total of sixteen feet in height and width. The curvature was such that there were no places to hide, and there were no sharp bends. Even as he dropped and acclimatized himself, the soldier was able to see

Ross in the distance, at the apex of a slow bend, gradually disappearing from view.

Taking the time to check his weapons, he made sure the Desert Eagle was loaded and that the Beretta had a full magazine. Other weapons hung from his combat harness: frag and stun grenades, extra ammo, and an AKSU, ready for the collapsible stock to be snapped into place. But for now, he'd stick with those weapons he favored most.

Bolan set off in pursuit of the three men. He took the outer curve of the pipe, so that he would get a good sighting on the curvature of his quarry when they came into view. He also ran a little way up the curve of the pipe, holding himself at an angle. It was tougher on the calf muscles, but allowed him to gain speed and distance on his prey while making less noise. His left foot lapped at the water, the right thudded on damp but uncovered concrete. It was his hope that the noise would be minimal, and covered from detection by the noise of those he pursued.

SIGNELLA WAS A TOUGH MAN, but not necessarily brave. He was no longer as drunk as he had been, and his fear was sharpening his reflexes as he moved. When he'd made his escape from the club, he hadn't dared to look back. He'd run as fast as he could, and had thought that he'd made the alley and slipped down into the storm drain without being heard. It was a route that he had been shown by Jean-Louis Garrault shortly after joining Destiny's Spear, and was one that the terrorists frequently used.

They were not the only ones to utilize the drains, and he knew that this would now work in his favor. His original intention had been to take the usual route back to base and warn the rest of the cell. But this had changed. How the hell they had gotten onto him he didn't know. When he'd shifted the manhole cover and then replaced it after him, he'd taken a look at the end of the alley, and there had been no one in sight.

But somehow they'd managed to trail him, and he could hear the noise they were making over the sound of his own splashing footsteps. He was sure there was more than one of them. The sounds of running in water were too recurrent, too overlapping for just one pair of feet. Was it the black guy and the lunatic redhead who were ready to waste him? Probably. But what if the dark guy who had first approached him was also on the trail? How the hell could he deal with three of them when he had no weapon?

There was only one thing he could do. He risked looking back over his shoulder to see how close they were. It was a mistake. He stumbled in the water, his feet slipping on the surface as soon as his attention was distracted. He could see them in the distance, gaining ground. Then they spiraled out of his vision as he tumbled and fell, turning a half somersault into the fetid water. His shoulder and head cracked painfully on the concrete beneath, the stench and taste of the brackish water going up his nose, into his startled and open mouth, making him choke and gag.

Ironically, the fall may have saved him. The redhead, probably irritated and bored with the chase, had decided to draw his Smith & Wesson .38 Special. As he ran he let loose a couple of shots in Signella's direction. The bullets passed over the space where Signella's body had been moments before, and whined as they ricocheted off the concrete of the drain, spilling dust and concrete chips into the sluggish stream.

Signella scrambled to his feet, the taste of stagnant water in his mouth replaced by the very real taste of fear, his tired limbs suddenly coordinated and infused with the desire to keep living. He heard the black guy yell at his companion. That may or may not stop the idiot from firing again Signella thought, but he didn't want to take bets on that. He had another plan.

He kept his head low and started to zigzag as he splashed through the water, tensed for the bullet that would take him out.

7

Bolan held the Beretta in front of him as he reached the bend in the storm drain. He heard the shots from Goldman—he recognized the sound of the Smith & Wesson .38—and cursed to himself. If the merc iced Signella, then the lead would be lost, and he would have to deal with the freelance agents before trying to pick up the trail again. It was getting far too messy. This should have been a simple trail and recover operation, but with these wild cards...

He could hear Ross's voice. "Jimmy!" the agent yelled. "What the hell are you doing?"

"He's away, Errol. What am I supposed to do?"

Bolan had to suppress a grim smile at the bitter humor of the reply. He slowed as the two men came into sight. Signella was nowhere to be seen, but as Goldman had whirled to face his partner, Bolan was coming right into his line of vision.

The soldier saw Goldman's surprise, but there was nothing wrong with the agent's reflexes as the Smith & Wesson was raised in his direction.

Bolan was quicker. He put a 3-round burst into the roof of the pipe between the two mercenaries. Ross, his back still to the Executioner, instinctively dived for cover, landing and rolling in the sluggish stream before coming up the right way.

"Oh great," he wailed as he realized the water had ruined his immaculate suit.

"Don't even think about it," Bolan shouted as Goldman sighted him. "I can take you both out before you have the chance to get one shell out of the chamber."

"Yeah? But what if—" Goldman began before Ross cut him short.

"Let it go, Jimmy. All the while we talk, Signella is getting away."

Goldman muttered something under his breath but raised both hands, palms out, so that the Smith & Wesson pointed to the roof of the pipe.

"That's good," Bolan said curtly. "Now for some answers, and quick. Where's Signella?"

Goldman inclined his head. "There's an inlet into the pipe up ahead that must lead into the sewage system. He's gone up that."

Bolan was sure that there was more to the underground tunnels of Marseilles than simply sewers. But Grimaldi was the one with the information, and he was off-line while they were this far down. He'd have to play this by ear.

"Then we follow," he said simply.

"Look, whoever you are, I'm with you on that, but can I assume it's safe for me to get up now without being ventilated?" Ross asked in a manner that veered between sardonic and peeved at the state of his suit.

"Yeah, but slowly, and hands away from the jacket," Bolan countered. "Meanwhile, Mr. Hot-tempered goes first—after putting the gun away—because he saw where Signella went. But slowly," he added as Goldman began to move.

"How can I do this slowly when we've got to follow someone who's gaining distance?" he grumbled.

"Because I don't trust you yet, and you can put on speed when the gun's out of the way," Bolan said calmly.

Ross, meanwhile was on his feet, and as Goldman climbed into the feeder tunnel up which Signella had scrambled, the black agent cast a look back over his shoulder.

"Look, my friend, we've got off to a bad start, but it occurs to me that the people I work for may just also be your paymasters."

"I don't think so," Bolan said, stopping in the middle of the pipe as Ross followed Goldman. "Now back up and stand with your hands above your heads," he added as the two mercs were in the smaller tunnel. "I don't want you to get ideas."

The soldier vaulted into the tunnel as the mercs stood well back, hands raised.

"Lead on, Goldman," Bolan said. "Which way?"

"Left," Goldman said, indicating the junction ahead with an inclination of his head. "And can I put my hands down now?"

"Yeah, as long as they're in plain sight," Bolan replied.

"One question. You know Jimmy's name, and—I assume—mine. So who are you? U.S. military, Justice Department, CIA or what?"

"My name is Matt Cooper," Bolan said simply. He didn't answer the other question. Instead he said, "Let's go."

The tunnels were getting smaller, and were made of crumbling brick shored up here and there by joists made of scrap wood tied and hammered together in varying thicknesses to join older sections of tunnel.

"There's another fork ahead, and I'm lost from there," Goldman said.

"You'd better not be lying to me," Bolan growled from the rear.

"Straight up," Goldman said in a genuinely aggrieved tone. "I only saw him go to the left back at the last turn."

"Then we're all equally in the dark. Well, well, spoke too soon," Ross murmured, as they hit the junction.

They were, indeed, no longer in the literal dark. Whatever else these tunnels may or may not have been, they were not sewers. And they were inhabited. These facts could be deduced from the evidence that the tunnels were dry, and were now lighted by a series of lights that were strung on the walls at regular intervals. Some were flashlights tied to stanchions, with the battery power in each of varying strengths. Every fifth or sixth torch, stretching in each direction from the junction, was made of sticks with kerosene soaked rags that burned at a low level, giving off a smoke that drifted in a breeze indicating an opening at each end onto fresher air.

Catacombs of some kind, Bolan thought. Many old towns and cities in southern France and in Spain had them beneath the town. The questions were, why were they being lit? Who was maintaining this light and for what reason?

All three men had been standing in silence for some while, listening intently to pick out any sound that may indicate the direction Signella had taken. What they heard was more disturbing. There were multiples of sound in each fork, footsteps and voices and other noises to indicate that the tunnels were in regular use.

"Cooper, I'm sure we're both working for the U.S. government in some way, and I'll bet we're not even after the same thing, so I'll cut you a deal," Ross whispered.

"There are no deals, Ross," Bolan replied in a low, level tone. "I've been sent after the chemical weapons that were taken. But I'll bet that wasn't the real reason for the robbery. There are rumors about a sonic weapon. I'll take a wild guess that's what you're after."

"You're a very well-informed man," Ross countered. "But you're only after the chemical weapons. The other is ours."

"We'll see."

"Cooper, we can't afford to screw around right now. Can we just call a truce until we're out of here, because I've got a real bad feeling about this. We've lost the Sicilian, and we don't know what we're about to come up against. We're going to need one another—or, at least, we could do without being at one another's throats until we're out of here."

"It would be mutually beneficial," Bolan said simply.

"Right, if the United Nations has stopped negotiating and come to some kind of agreement, can we get on with it?" Goldman said irritably.

"You'll have to excuse my partner, he can be a little volatile," Ross said wryly.

"I think I may have gathered that," Bolan replied. "Which way, then?"

"There are more noises down here," Goldman indicated. "I figure Signella's turning up might have stirred up whatever's going on here. Or else there's just more activity."

"That's what I like about you, you're so perceptive," Ross mused sarcastically.

"Well, what's your suggestion, then?" Goldman said heatedly.

Bolan looked back the way they had come and made a quick calculation. "I think we should follow Goldman's suggestion," he said. "The area with the greater activity follows the direction of the storm drain, down toward the docks. I had an idea that Destiny's Spear might be based that way, maybe keeping the merchandise down there with them."

"It'd figure," Ross agreed. "The noise could be a bunch of dubious characters indulging in a little thieving and smuggling, which would account for why they would keep these tunnels well lit."

"Great. Now we've finished admiring one another's intuitive perception, perhaps we can move?" Goldman whispered. "And another thing. If there's danger ahead, I want my gun in my hand."

"No, no hardware unless necessary. The state of these tunnels, any loose fire could cause a cave-in," Bolan stated. He didn't add that he didn't trust Goldman to hold that fire if his temper frayed any more.

"Then you put that Beretta away as well, or we don't go anywhere," Goldman said calmly, fixing Bolan with a stare that was assessing the way the Executioner reacted.

Bolan needed their trust for now. He nodded and holstered the Beretta on his blacksuit's web belt, now clearly visible as the shirt had become ripped and torn in the chase.

A small smile crossed Goldman's lips. "Okay, let's do it," he said.

The three men set off in the direction of the greatest noise, leading them down toward the docks. The tunnel was thicker with smoke as they moved among the torches, the accumulation of the torches filling the tunnel with the stench of kerosene and burning material. But the air was still breathable, and the breeze that carried the fresh air through was now stronger, so that they could feel it on their faces.

The tunnels were a maze, with a number of crisscrossing corridors of old stone that took them off at obtuse angles from their main direction, but always leading them back toward the right direction as they followed the growing noise.

"What have we stumbled into?" Ross breathed as he and Goldman rounded a corner and came to an enclave that had been carved out of the tunnel. Bolan, a few steps behind them, was taken aback by the tone of the merc's voice until he came within sight of what had inspired it.

At a point where the tunnels had converged, those who used them had, at one point, hollowed out the junction, pushing back the walls until they had made a large room that was no higher than the roofs of the surrounding tunnels, but now consisted of a circular hall. The ceilings had been shored up by a series of joists and pillars that stood in the hall.

But it was not this bizarre construction that had caused all three men to come to a complete halt. Rather, it was the nature of the people who filled the room. Scattered across the floor, around three small bonfires that did nothing to detract from the smokiness of the atmosphere, was a motley collection of males and females, young and old. The homeless, the alcoholic and the dispossessed, many of them looked as though it had been some time since they had seen daylight, so pale were they beneath the grime that covered them.

Only a few of them noticed the entrance of the three men. And of those who did, not many were in any condition to do any more than just stare.

"So this is where the drunks, junkies and the lazy sink to, is it?" Goldman said, spitting on the floor. "Christ, they don't look like any smugglers or terrorists to me. Looks like we've been down the wrong path this time."

Bolan remembered what "Mickey" had told him in the club before the action had kicked off. He could well imagine how easy it was to seek refuge beneath the streets. And also what a good cover it could provide.

"I don't think we have," he said quietly. "This would be a perfect cover. We should ask a few questions."

"What kind of answers are we going to get from these people?" Ross said with a despair that differed from his partner's contempt. "They're too far into their own little worlds to be coherent."

"Not necessarily," Bolan replied, casting his eyes around the room. He picked out a man huddled against the wall to his right. His eyes were bright and focused, and he was making himself conspicuous, ironically, by his very attempts to press himself back into the wall and appear invisible.

The Executioner turned and walked slowly the few yards between them. The man was of an indeterminate age, Bolan pinning it down to under forty. He was also frozen in fear as he watched Bolan approach.

So far, the three men had been speaking to one another in English. Bolan couldn't tell if the man had understood, or was terrified simply because he couldn't understand. Bolan was framing a simple question in French, smiling in a gesture of friendship that softened the derelict's frozen rigidity, when Goldman exploded, changing everything.

8

It was the scream that first distracted Bolan. High-pitched, whining and with a note of complete terror. At almost the exact same moment, the man he had been about to question whimpered and turned his head away, as though he expected the same thing to happen to him.

Bolan turned and saw Goldman holding one of the derelicts up by the rags he was dressed in, hitting him in the gut.

"Don't ignore me, just tell me if you saw him," the redhead yelled in excruciatingly bad French. So bad that, in truth, Bolan was doubtful that the merc's victim could understand him in his terror and his drunken state.

"Jimmy—" Ross said, moving toward Goldman, but Bolan was past him before he had a chance to take more than a couple of steps.

The soldier grabbed the redhead by the shoulder, spinning him and punching him in his jaw. The merc dropped his victim and dropped onto the filthy ground.

"Cooper, what the hell—" Ross began before Bolan whirled on him. The burning anger in the soldier's eyes silenced Ross before he could say anything else.

"Listen," Bolan snapped, turning his attention to Goldman,

stronger

ward the

o-back,

of the

nding

on the

mber

long

ht to

em.

eo-

oss

ad

s,

...aking his head slowly to try to clear ...people we're after, and beating on them ...y answers."

...urry things up," Goldman grumbled. ...ing to do it?" Bolan said, casting an eye ...e done is given us a lot of trouble."

...of fear had dropped from the derelicts, and ...had been in a stupor were now awakened and ...ad been going on around them. There was a ...f muttering, and on the edges of the chamber, ...rting to group together. Bottles discarded in a ...e were now taken up as weapons, flaming tim- ...om the bonfires. There was the dull glint of knives, ...or sharp as the Tekna Bolan carried, but sharp ...o cut.

...n took the Tekna from where it was sheathed on the ...uit's harness. "Looks like we've got trouble," he said ...y. "You'd better be ready to fight your way out of this, ...lman."

We can just blast our way through," Ross said, pulling the Beretta half out of its holster. He stopped when he caught the grim expression on Bolan's face.

"You draw that, and I'll break your arm and then your neck," Bolan whispered with a hard-edged tone that would brook no argument. "Our fight is not with these people."

"Yeah, but theirs is with us," Goldman snapped, scrambling to his feet.

"And if you start firing down here, then we lose all chance of trailing Signella," Bolan continued, ignoring the redhead. "The sound is going to travel all through these tunnels. No, we do this by hand."

While they had been arguing, the men and women in the

chamber had banded into small groups, growing
and surer in their numbers. They began to advance to
trio of agents. Bolan, Ross and Goldman stood back-
forming a circle. They had moved toward the center
chamber to give themselves a better view of the surro
area. The torches and bonfires cast a flickering light
stones, making the shadows in the corners of the cha
jump wildly. Anything or anyone could be in those. As
as they stayed central, then there would be enough lig
see whoever came at them.

Bolan's eyes flickered over the groups surrounding th
He estimated there were between twenty-five to thirty p
ple in the chamber. Almost ten to one. Not good odds. R
and Goldman were using their bare hands, while Bolan h
the Tekna. Their opponents were mostly armed with knive
bottles and flaming wood. It was a far from fair fight. Bu
on the balancing side, these were street people, eithe
derelict, drunk, drugged or just wasted through living rough
Armed as they were, they should be no match for three
men who had trained for combat and had to live on the edge
of violence every day. If they could avoid being caught by
any of the weapons, then they had a better than fighting
chance.

There was a tense pause, as the groupings around them
waited for someone to make the first move. The trio held back,
waiting to see from where the first attack would stem. Finally,
the tension became too great for one of the derelicts, who
screamed hysterically and ran forward, waving his blunt blade
before him.

His target was Goldman, who parried the thrust with his
forearm, the blade sliding off the sleeve of his leather jacket,
and returned with a vicious chop to the throat that cut his op-

ponent down immediately, the man falling to the floor, choking heavily as he writhed in the dirt.

The floodgates were opened. The outcasts streamed forward in groups. Ross, near one of the fires and seeing a glowing timber still in the remains, stooped with a lithe grace to pick it up with one hand, waving it like a baton on the upward sweep of his arm. The glowing charcoaled end of the wood caught three attackers across the face and arms, causing them to yell in agony and fall back, cannoning into those behind them in their panic, and causing them to tumble to the floor.

Bolan, for his part, was unwilling to use the Tekna unless necessary. He waited for the first of those tackling him to get near, then pivoted on his left heel, his right leg coming out and the heavy heel of his combat boot taking three of the oncoming across their chests as he arced. They fell back into their companions, taking out some of the more unsteady by default.

Both feet on the ground, his balance restored, he found that a vanguard was now upon him. They swarmed over him, waving bottles and pieces of wood that were no longer flaming, but were still red hot at their burned ends. There was also a carving knife with a chunk from the dulled side of the blade missing that he could see flashing in the air.

Breathing deeply and evenly, he saw the panic, fear and anger of those attacking him. The only real threat from them was if one of the bottles or the knives should strike a telling blow. They were weak and ineffectual as fighters, and all he had to do was immobilize them one by one. The knifeman, carving the air, was the first. A jab took the man in the chest, the power of Bolan's forearm and biceps muscles driving his adversary backward. On the return, a whiplash movement to the right took out a woman with a broken wine bottle, her head lashing back under the impact and catching another assailant under the chin.

Shifting his balance, Bolan used the handle of the Tekna to send another opponent into oblivion. Those who were left were now beginning to have second thoughts about taking on the soldier, and some had already scattered into the darkness of the tunnels surrounding the chamber.

To his left and right, Ross and Goldman were also dealing with their assailants. Under the expensive, though now badly soiled and rumpled suit, Ross packed a formidable set of muscles. He had both speed and strength, which he demonstrated now as he swung the piece of red-hot wood as though it were a nunchaku, keeping those attacking him at a fearful distance until he had formed a plan of attack. He danced forward and kicked out at the nearest derelict. Pivoting on the balls of his feet, he turned and threw the red-hot wood at the next attacker, making the man flinch. Ross took advantage of this distraction to jab at the guy's jaw, hitting him on the point and making him drop to the dirt. Bolan watched as classic boxing moves handled another three attackers, before a fourth came at him from an oblique angle. Ross saw the man move forward from the corner of his eye, and shot out a foot that took the man on the side of his knee. The iron-hard blow made him crumble to one side, and the merc brought his foot down hard on the man's wrist, forcing him to loosen his grip on the broken bottle he was holding. A two-footed shuffle, and a swift kick under the chin shut out the lights in the man's eyes.

Goldman was faring less well. The redhead's temper had been a problem, and Bolan was right to surmise that this loose cannon would be a major problem. Screaming and yelling his frustration at the delay as he laid into the group converging on him, he was proving to be the consummate streetfighter, kicking, punching and gouging at those who got near enough, a whirling dervish ball of energy. He was also proving to be tough, taking blows from lumps of wood and the occasional thrown bottle without flinching, despite the blood that was streaming from a cut opened up above his hairline.

But if he was a consummate streetfighter, he also suffered from the downside of this art. He was undisciplined, and concentrated solely on one or two opponents, allowing others to get under his guard. Where Bolan, and even Ross, could step back and look at the bigger picture while they tackled an opponent, Goldman was far too focused by his own anger. So he was slowly being overwhelmed by the numbers rather than the power of his opponents.

It was at this point that his temper, flaring redder than his hair or the blood streaming down his face could ever have been, came to the fore, and he forgot the words Bolan had spoken when they knew they would have to stand and fight. Taking a step back, roaring his fury, Goldman dipped his hand into his jacket and took out the Smith & Wesson .38 Special. Without pausing, he pointed it at the oncoming face of a young woman who held a flick knife.

"Fuck you. Fuck the lot of you," he yelled angrily, squeezing the trigger.

The shot sounded like the toll of a giant bell within the enclosed chamber, stopping all action for a fraction of a second. The target of the attack never had a chance to register the shock on her face, as it was eradicated by the slug, which entered at the bridge of her nose, the bullet deflected by the septum so that it exited at the rear of her skull at an angle that sprayed bone, blood and brain in a fine shower over those behind her.

This turn of events was too much for those who were still upright. The crowd split and fled down the tunnels, shouting and screaming, falling over one another in their fear and their haste to get away from the next shot. The only ones left in the chamber were those who were either barely conscious and unable to move or those still unconscious from the fray.

"Oh, well done, Jimmy, you idiot," Ross rasped in the ensuing silence.

Bolan turned angrily on the redhead, regardless of the fact that he was armed.

"What? What did I do?" Goldman asked in a frustrated voice before the soldier had a chance to speak. "She had a knife and she was gonna do me. What was I supposed to do, let her have me rather than make a noise?"

"You could have brought down the roof in here," Bolan snapped, looking up dubiously at the precarious construction, "and you've sure as hell alerted anyone else down here that we're around."

Goldman shrugged and was about to speak when Bolan held up a hand—the one still clutching the Tekna—to stop him.

"Listen... Movement, and it's coming this way."

While the departing outcasts had made so little noise scurrying away to hide in the far-flung tunnels of the catacombs, there was no mistaking the sounds of running feet coming from the direction of the docks.

Bolan pulled out the AKSU, checking the magazine and snapping back the stock on the shortened but still powerful version of the AK-74. Cradling it in the crook of his arm, he also took out the Beretta.

"I'd advise you to do the same, gentlemen," he said as he moved, "because I don't reckon we're going to have to find Signella. I think he's coming to find us, and bringing some friends with him."

While Goldman and Ross reloaded and checked their own weapons, aware that they had a limited supply of ammunition with no idea what they were facing, the Executioner had decided that it was time for him to take the offensive.

Five tunnels led off the chamber—two in the direction from which they had come, one seemingly leading off to nowhere at one side and two that took them toward the dockside areas that Bolan was sure were the reason these tunnels were still in use. The way he figured it, gangs of thieves and smugglers would use the tunnels, and the terrorists—no strangers themselves to robbery with violence—could use this activity as cover for their operations, perhaps taking part in it themselves as a trade-off. Which meant that he, Ross and Goldman would be up against not just the terrorists, but any other criminals who happened to be around, and who could be armed.

Time to do a recon, and maybe to cut off their options in order to give himself and the mercenaries as much of an advantage as they could hope for.

Swiftly and silently, the soldier moved across to the two tunnels that led to the dock area. The first he scouted ran for about a hundred yards before curving away sharply to the left. It was from this direction that the enemy appeared to be approaching, fast. Holstering the Beretta for a moment, he produced a grenade from its container strung on the blacksuit's combat harness. He pulled the pin, holding down the spoon as he judged the distance between himself and the approaching horde. He released the spoon and tossed the grenade at the angle of the curve. It hit the ground at the tightest angle of the wall and rolled around the corner. He saw this as he backed away rapidly, covering the empty corridor with the AKSU in the event of any enemy making it before the blast.

Bolan backed into the chamber. "Down the right. Move it!" he yelled, leading the way into the right-hand tunnel. Ross and Goldman followed without question, but both were taken by surprise when the grenade detonated. Their ears felt as though they were about to burst from the pressure. Although Bolan had taken the precaution of opening his mouth to equalize the pressure, he still felt the pain of the blast within the tight and confined space. The force of the explosion drove dust and brick segments out from the tunnel into the empty chamber, blowing out the flame torches. All three men were thrown to the dirt by the shake of the ground and the force of the blast.

Behind them, in the sudden silence that followed the aftershock, Bolan heard the rumble of the chamber ceiling begin to collapse. The ramshackle construction that was keeping the roof aloft could never have stood up to the blast.

Bolan got to his feet and shouted at Ross and Goldman. "Come on, time to move."

"I thought you didn't want to make any noise or risk bringing the ceiling down," Goldman muttered as he got to his feet, shaking his head and still seeming dazed by what had happened.

"That was then," Bolan snapped. "Your action has brought them running, so now we take the initiative. Some of them are dead, and the tunnel is blocked. This must link up farther back down the system, so they'll have to use this, and we'll be ready for them. So do you want to stop asking stupid questions?"

"Let's get to it," Ross said, cutting through his partner's belligerence with a crisp efficiency. "You're in charge. Tell us what to do."

Bolan took a look at the tunnel. With his ears ringing, it was difficult to tell if any of the enemy was nearly on them.

"Wait here," he snapped, taking the distance between their location and the angle of the tunnel in a few swift strides. He flattened himself against the wall of the curve and then risked a look around, the AKSU ready to fire. The tunnel stretched into the darkness, where a number of torches had been snuffed, so he was unable to get a really clear picture. But one thing was for sure—the enemy was approaching, as he could hear them over the ringing that was still in his ears.

He backed up.

"They're on their way. Can't see how many, but it sounds like more than half a dozen. Follow me and listen carefully…and you may need these," he added, picking some 9 mm clips from his combat harness and handing them to Ross as they ran. He then took the Desert Eagle from its holster and handed it to Goldman, along with some spare clips. "Backup for you. Look after it well," he said.

The three men took up their positions, Bolan knocking out the two torches nearest the angle of the tunnel curve. In the darkness around that curve, the enemy had slowed, wary of running into traps. Bolan and Ross had weapons that could do a lot of damage. With his Smith & Wesson revolver alone, Goldman couldn't contribute much to the fight, but the Desert Eagle gave him at least a kind of parity with firepower.

"They're in sight," Bolan whispered, risking a look around the curve and into the darkness. He trusted that the torches he had knocked out would provide enough cover for him not to be seen. The lack of fire suggested he was correct. But he could see them, coming into view.

"Okay, now, and remember to keep in sequence," he whispered, pulling back long enough to give the command.

"Aye-aye, Captain," Ross said grimly, taking a deep breath and springing into action.

The mercenary swung out into the corridor, blasting Beretta fire in an arc across the face of the oncoming opposition. The speed of his action was enough to insure that return fire was sluggish to begin with, and two men in the front of the enemy attack went down with lines stitched across chest and abdomen. Stray return fire whined off the brickwork around him, but he stood his ground, ignoring it.

While he did this, Goldman moved out, keeping low and fast. He settled against the opposite wall to his partner, to prevent cluster fire from the enemy, and began to blast with the Smith & Wesson. He was soon out of ammo and shoved the revolver into his jacket pocket as he leveled the Desert Eagle and began to fire. The .44 Magnum pistol was like a cannon compared to the .38 Special, and the initial impact almost unbalanced him. But he managed to keep the gun down, and adjusted his weight and balance to the kickback from the heavy, Israeli-made weapon. He knew that he would have to stick with this, as the constant reloading of the Smith & Wesson was almost an impossibility. Replacing the clips in the Desert Eagle was a much faster process.

With Ross and Goldman established, and providing cover, Bolan moved into action. The Executioner cut between them, keeping low and cradling the AKSU as he sought a forward position. Throwing himself flat and rolling to the wall under Ross's line of fire, he brought the AKSU up against his shoulder and began to pump out rounds in the direction of the retreating enemy. In front of him, marking the point at which the action had begun, were the two corpses that Ross had claimed with his first bursts.

Bolan heard the chatter of the Beretta cease, and he stood, still firing, to provide cover for Ross as he advanced down the tunnel. When Ross was in position, flat to the ground to allow Bolan to fire over his head, Goldman made his next advance.

They were moving rapidly down the tunnel, and had now reached the point where the torches had been extinguished. Sweat spangled Bolan's brow as he strained his eyes to acclimate to the darkness, not wanting to fire at his own people or miss any opposition that may be using the darkness to make an ambush.

But there seemed to be no opposition in view. The return fire no longer whined on the brickwork around, and it seemed as though the enemy had just retreated into the catacombs.

"Cease fire," the soldier yelled over the chatter of the Beretta and the echoing roar of the Desert Eagle. He figured that the darkness would provide a reasonable camouflage to prevent the enemy picking them out.

As the sounds of the gunfire died, he strained his ears to pick out any noise the enemy may be making. There was little. It seemed to him that they had turned tail and fled in panic. Somewhere in the distance he could hear the sound of people moving, possibly an evac.

"I think they're moving out," he whispered. "Double-time. Follow the noise and watch any side tunnels to make sure."

The three men set off at speed, weapons reloaded and ready to fire. They needed to make time in order to reach the enemy before they deserted the catacombs, yet at the same time it was imperative that they didn't fall prey to an ambush.

So they moved forward in the same manner as they had before, but without laying down covering fire. They came across four subsidiary tunnels leading off from their direction, three to the right-hand side and one to the left. In each case, a quick burst from the Beretta or the AKSU neutralized any threat, although it seemed unlikely that any lay in those dark spaces.

The noise in front of them grew stronger. They were approaching the area where the enemy was based. Throughout the action, they hadn't caught sight of Signella, but there was little doubt in any of their minds that he was involved with the action. He had come this way because it was where Destiny's Spear was located.

The only problem was that their target knew they were coming. The necessity to spray fire down the adjacent corridors as cover meant that their approach was clearly audible—and their progress easy to judge. The lighting in this section of the old catacombs was good, with high-wattage bulbs and strong batteries powering the flashlights. This would make them all-too-easy to see.

Bolan pulled up as they approached another tunnel curve. He flattened himself against the wall and beckoned his comrades to do likewise.

"Now we've got a problem," he said softly. "By the amount of noise they're making, I'd figure that they're just around the corner, and you can bet that they'll have sentries posted and waiting for us. If we go straight in, we're dead."

"Then what do you suggest we do, sit here and wait?" Goldman asked with barely disguised sarcasm.

Bolan ignored his tone, treating it as a serious question. "We can't. They're in the process of moving out, and I'd figure that half the gendarmerie in Marseilles will be on our ass before long. The shooting and the grenade have certainly drawn attention. We're not that far underground that it wouldn't have been noticed up above."

"So time is of the essence. I suggest we make a maneuver like before and go in blazing. It worked then." Ross shrugged.

Bolan considered that. Shaking his head, he said, "It's risky. If we hit those chemical weapons and shatter the flasks, then we've unleashed certain death for miles around. We've got to be more cautious." A slow smile crossed his face. "Yeah, it might just work," he said almost to himself. "Listen, you guys count to fifty and then start to lay down some fire. Very minor, just enough to draw their attention and let them know we're here. Just enough to keep them focused."

"And you?" Ross queried.

"Just trust me, and move when you hear the roar," the soldier said, patting the AKSU before moving back up the tunnel the way they'd come.

Goldman gave Ross a bemused stare, but the merc just shrugged at his partner, and started to count in a whisper: "One…two…three…"

Bolan moved back up the corridor as far as the last off-shoot tunnel. He knew it was clear as they had fired a precautionary blast down it on passing. He also figured that there was little chance of anyone in the main enemy camp keeping a guard on it. They thought that the opposing force was headed straight, and the probing fire from Ross and Goldman would reinforce that view.

It was exactly what he wanted.

The tunnel was dark. It had obviously been lit entirely by torches, which had been extinguished by the blowout from the earlier grenade blast. Bolan slowed and felt his way cautiously along the passage, one hand outstretched on the wall to grope along and keep flush to the side.

His hand hit air. A turnoff. He could hear the sounds of evac coming from that direction. He moved around to stay flush to the wall as he took off down this new tunnel. The brickwork curved and ahead he could see a dullish light. The noises were louder now.

The curve of the corridor obviously emerged into the chamber where the terrorists, and whoever else they worked with, had their base. By the look of the illumination, the chamber was near. And it seemed that they had not deemed it worthwhile to place a guard at the entrance, as the illumination was even, with nobody to block some of the light.

This was the entrance Bolan had been hoping for. While the terrorists continued their evac and returned the sporadic fire from Ross and Goldman on the other side of the chamber, they would be completely unprepared for what was about to happen.

All the while, Bolan had been counting in his head: "Forty-six...forty-seven...forty-eight...forty-nine..."

On the count of fifty, the Executioner moved into action.

Pushing off from the wall against which he had been resting, he came around the curve of the tunnel with the AKSU firing into the chamber's entrance. But he still had to be somewhat cautious and reduce the risk of breaking the chemical flasks if they were in the room. The only way to do that was to hit hard, find direct targets and to strike with surprise, preventing the enemy from firing back and setting up a siege situation. There was still a chance of the flasks being broken, but this way it was much reduced.

Unloading continuous rounds as he moved, Bolan finally got his first look at the place where the terrorists had made their base.

The room, hollowed out of the catacombs, was about

twenty feet square, and the first thing he noticed was that the only weapons in sight were those in or near the hands of the people in the room. One part of his brain breathed a sigh of relief. He had been hoping that they would keep living and briefing quarters separate from their armory, or else he and the mercs ran the risk of setting off a giant bomb below ground. The rest of his mind was focused on the task ahead.

As he advanced, pumping fire into the chamber, he took a note of who was there.

Signella was holding an Uzi, with blood staining a makeshift dressing applied to his lower left arm. Probably a superficial wound, perhaps a nick from the fire in the tunnel or a splinter of wood or brickwork. It didn't seem to be impeding him. There was a small, elfin woman with an AKSU that dwarfed her hands, and a tall, thin bearded man with an H&K MP-5. Two men stood near what had to be the entrance to the tunnel from which Ross and Goldman were firing. One had an Uzi, the other an MP-5, and they were firing sporadically into the darkness, returning the fire from the mercenaries.

Seven other people were in the room, three men, four women. They had weapons on shoulder straps, but they were too busy packing papers and belongings to have them at hand. It was an evac, all right. They wanted to leave no sign, no clue behind them, and their haste had made them careless.

The shells from Bolan's AKSU ripped across the room. Signella, the bearded man and the woman all dived for whatever cover they could find, lifting their weapons to return fire. For the two men covering the other entrance, there wasn't enough time to react and move. The AKSU rounds ripped across the middle of their bodies, almost separating torso from abdomen as they both tried to turn and return fire. Last nerve-twitch reactions sent Uzi fire into the ceiling of the chamber, bringing down dust and dirt, obscuring the view.

Bolan stepped into the room and sought immediate cover, wondering if Ross and Goldman had started their advance.

"I MAKE IT FIFTY," Goldman said impatiently.

"You're counting too fast," Ross whispered, only up to forty-three in his head.

"So who says how fast you have to count?" Goldman shrugged. "I just want to get going."

"Now let's go," Ross countered, having reached fifty in his own head. "I just hope Cooper counts at the same speed, or we're chopped liver."

Goldman reloaded the Desert Eagle and rose to his feet from his previous crouch.

Pumping out covering fire, the two men emerged from the angle of the corridor and turned the corner, heading for the light. The noises within the room were interrupted by the volcanic blast of controlled AKSU fire, and they saw the two guards with whom they had been exchanging fire suddenly jerk and fall, their bodies almost ruptured by the heavy-duty assault rifle shells.

Ross grinned and held his fire as he and his partner gained the entrance to the chamber and saw the mayhem within. They just had a glimpse of their partner as he took cover, and noted that there were ten other fighters in the room. Three had weapons in hand, and were turning to focus on the Executioner. Seven others were in the process of scrambling for their arms.

Not if Ross and Goldman could help it.

The three men and four women didn't stand a chance. A

burst from the Beretta took them in neat lines from throat to groin, the high-impact 9 mm rounds rupturing organs and causing fatal damage in seconds. Those who didn't succumb to the Beretta found large holes blasted in their bodies by the .44 Magnum rounds of the Desert Eagle. They hardly had time to react before their lives were taken from them.

In terms of possible harm to the chemical flasks, it was a case of maximum impact, minimum danger. All fire from the mercs had been directed at the bodies of their enemies, and the surrounding chamber was relatively untouched.

Their part was done.

THE SOLDIER KNEW there was little cover, and in drawing the fire from the mercs, he was endangering himself. But it had to be done. After his initial burst, he had noticed that there were packing cases to his right. They would provide little in the way of protection, but using them for cover may just buy him that vital fraction of a second.

As he hit the ground behind them, twisting as quickly as possible in the confined space, he heard and felt Uzi and MP-5 gunfire splinter the wood above him, thudding into the brick wall above his head, showering him with dust. He had only a few seconds until they lowered their aim enough to take him out.

The rain of shells above him faltered. He heard other fire, including the unmistakable booming of the Desert Eagle, and he knew that Ross and Goldman had followed his cue.

Bolan took advantage of the stutter to make his move. Coming up smoothly, he took out the elfin woman and the bearded man with two short bursts. As the shells hit and their bodies twisted toward him, recognition hit. They were the faces of Jean-Louise Garrault and Francine Malpas, from the photos of Destiny's Spear.

They both hit the ground, dead. In the sudden lull of fire, this left Signella between Bolan on one side, and Ross and Goldman on the other. The Sicilian gazed wildly at his three opponents, not knowing what to do.

"Give it up, Signella," Bolan commanded. "You help us, you get to live."

Signella turned instinctively at the soldier's words. As he turned, the Uzi moved upward, but Bolan could see that his finger had relaxed on the trigger.

Goldman shot him.

9

"Konstantin! Konstantin! For God's sakes, move your ass and get in here."

The cabin door opened, and Hector Chavez-Smith's personal bodyguard stepped into the room. He was breathing heavily, as though he had run to respond to the call.

"What's going on out there?" Chavez-Smith demanded. He was seated at his desk in his private quarters on the yacht, dressed only in a bathrobe. Two thick lines of cocaine were divided on the blotter in front of him, and he was using a hundred-dollar bill to snort them. His nose tingled and itched, the powder searing tissues already long since scarred by constant use. The amount he had consumed in that evening was enough to tilt him over the edge, making him paranoid and tense. He had wanted the Countess D'Orsini to stay, even asked her, and the bitch declined. And now he was alone, with no bimbo in sight to satisfy him. This was not helping his temper.

All of this went through his mind as he waited for his bodyguard to reply. As with all the man's speech, it was clipped and heavily accented.

"Trouble in town. Someone setting off explosives beneath the sewer. Many police gathering. Nothing to directly affect us."

Chavez-Smith furrowed his brow. As far as this idiot knew, that was correct. But Signella and Destiny's Spear had established a base in the catacombs, trading off arms with the smuggling crews for the rights to use some of their underground territory. Even if the terrorists weren't involved with the events beneath the town, the incursion of the police could have dire effects.

"What about Signella? Have you seen him this evening?"

The bodyguard shrugged. "Before sundown. He say he go after his woman."

Chavez-Smith nodded slowly and dismissed the bodyguard with a wave. But as the man reached the cabin door, the arms dealer called out.

"Better prepare to cast off at short notice. Just a precaution," he said before once more gesturing dismissively.

"I SHOULD SHOOT YOU NOW, before you cause any more problems," Bolan said angrily, leveling the AKSU at Goldman.

"Easy, big man, easy," Ross said quickly, palms up to show that he meant no threat. "The idiot is my partner, let me deal with him."

Before either Bolan or Goldman had a chance to respond, Ross turned and hit Goldman across the face with the barrel of the Beretta. The redhead, taken completely off guard and unable to protect himself from the force of the blow, went sprawling across the blood encrusted dirt floor.

"He's right, he should shoot you!" Ross yelled. "What the fuck did you do that for, Jimmy?"

Goldman sat up, eyes clouded, and spit a gob of bloody phlegm onto the already saturated floor beside him. The room stank of cordite and blood, the smells of violent death. The pause before Goldman spoke gave them a chance to realize the stench was amplified by the enclosed underground space.

"'Course I shot the bastard, he was pointing the gun at him," he said in a dazed but calm voice, indicating Bolan.

"He had his finger away from the trigger and was about to give it up," Bolan said between clenched teeth, his patience almost exhausted. "We needed him alive, not dead. What can he tell us now?"

"I didn't know, did I…" The voice of the still-stunned Goldman trailed off.

Bolan slung the AKSU over his shoulder and moved out into the middle of the carnage.

"Okay, forget it for now. We need to see if there's anything they left behind before the police get here."

"I'm with you," Ross said briefly, and the two men began to search the chamber while Goldman sat dazed, gradually returning to his senses.

The packing cases and boxes that had been filled to move out of the chamber revealed very little. Wherever their armory was, it was either in a different part of the catacombs or in another location entirely, as there was nothing to indicate a weapons cache, and no noise of activity to indicate that there was anyone else in the tunnels at the moment. They knew that they had to work quickly, however, and both men sifted through the cases with a quick-fingered efficiency. Most of the material consisted of personal effects that would identify Destiny's Spear members, or papers relating to planned actions. But finally Ross uncovered something that didn't fit with the rest of the material.

"Cooper, look at this," he said, turning to Bolan.

The soldier left his own search and joined Ross, examining the package the merc handed to him. It was a wrapped parcel. The tape around it had been cut and then resealed.

Bolan carefully unwrapped it once again, taking off the insulating and protective packaging until he came to a box. The computerized lock had not been set, and with a sinking heart he opened the lid.

Inside were three flasks, all still sealed, all seemingly untouched. There was also a pouch that was empty.

Bolan breathed a sigh of relief. "The chemical weapons. They didn't have a chance to hand them over to Chavez-Smith."

"Yeah, but that wasn't *really* what he was after, was it?" Ross remarked ruefully, studying the case. He reached out and opened up the empty pouch. "It's already gone."

"The sonic weapon?" Bolan stated.

"That's what we're after," Ross replied simply. "They must have already taken it to Chavez-Smith. All this for nothing," he added, shaking his head. "Man, I really thought it would be Signella who'd be the carrier."

"Maybe that's what we were supposed to think," Bolan mused softly. "Intel would have Signella as the contact, so anyone on the trail would pick him up immediately. To use him as a decoy makes perfect sense." His attention shifted to the empty pouch. "How can a sonic weapon be that small?" he asked. "It'd have to be bigger, just to—"

"No, man, that's the beauty of it," Ross interrupted. "These people who've hired us are years ahead of what they let the rest of your military know. When we were briefed, they didn't tell us how it worked, but they had to tell us what we were looking for. It's a microchip and the circuitry and programming on it can take any home PC and turn the speakers on it into a weapon. It's the ultimate portable weapon when it comes to sonics. Anything that runs on a computer system can be adapted in a matter of minutes."

"And let me guess—the chip will be easy to reproduce

once Chavez-Smith or whoever he's dealing with has the chance to take it apart and examine it."

"They didn't say for sure, but I'd guess that's about the size of it, and that's why they're panicking so much."

Bolan said nothing as he secured the flasks in their case, bound it in the protective layer and stowed it in a secure pouch on his combat harness. When this was done, he spoke. "Then I guess the best place to start looking for it is on Chavez-Smith's yacht. Let's go—"

"What do you mean, let's go?" Ross said slowly, his voice showing an edge of hostility that had not been there a moment before.

"I mean let's get Chavez-Smith and try to recover this chip."

"No, man, I don't think you get it. Your job is done. They only wanted you to get back the chemical weapons. And now you have them." He indicated the safely stowed case. "You get to go back to your paymasters and tell them it's done, while we go after our target. It's that simple."

"It isn't. That black project isn't so black anymore. There's been light on it, and some details have got out. The man in the Oval Office will want it, so it can be on official record. That brings it into my domain."

"Cooper, I don't want to fall out with you over this, but it's not just about me, you and Jimmy," Ross said. "The people we work for will expect us to take you out and reclaim it ourselves, rather than share."

"And you reckon you could take me out?" Bolan said, fixing Ross with a hard stare.

It was a tense moment that seemed to go on forever. Ross tried to hold the stare, but it was impossible. Bolan was a driven man, driven by his principles, and a sense of purpose and duty that could never allow him to back down. Ross could read all of that in the soldier's clear, icy-blue eyes. He looked away.

"Guess that's their problem, not mine," he said softly.

"What about mine?" Goldman asked, now on his feet and gradually returning to a grip on reality.

"You just shut up and follow," Ross snapped. "You've nearly blown this out of the water too often to have an opinion."

"I think we'd better get the hell out of here as soon as possible," Bolan said, "before the police get down here and before Chavez-Smith gets away."

CHAVEZ-SMITH WAS still seated at his desk when he heard the gentle knocking at his cabin door.

"Come," he commanded, and turned to see his bodyguard enter with the whip-thin and nervous Emil Herve.

"He comes from Signella," the bodyguard said brusquely before leaving them alone at an indication from his chief.

Herve stood nervously for a few seconds, before Chavez-Smith snapped, "Well? Why are you here?"

Herve sighed and closed his eyes, as though summoning up the words he was about to speak.

"Salvatore is probably dead by now. So are Jean-Louis and Francine, although that will be no loss. I am the only one left from the raid, and so Salvatore entrusted it to me before setting up the rearguard action."

"What rearguard action, and entrusted you with what?" Chavez-Smith inquired, leaning forward.

"Three men tried to take Salvatore at the Noir, and there was a firefight. He thought he had escaped, but they followed him into the catacombs. They fought hard, and they blew out great chunks of the tunnels. The gendarmes are everywhere, and it's chaos out there. The three men got as far as our base, as we were trying to evacuate. Salvatore gave me the weapon you wanted us to steal, entrusted me with bringing it to you. I left them there. For all I know, they may be dead."

"Everyone?" Chavez-Smith asked incredulously.

"Of those there," Herve replied with a shrug. "Not everyone was at base."

"Where are the others?" Chavez-Smith asked. He was now on his feet and restlessly pacing the cabin.

"Probably their usual haunts. There were only eleven of us down in the catacombs."

Chavez-Smith nodded. Destiny's Spear was a cell nearly thirty strong. So two-thirds were still on the loose, although their loyalty to him was compromised with Signella out of the picture.

"Very well. Find them, spread word that we are to regroup at the château. And I will take the weapon," he added as Herve turned to leave.

The thin terrorist paused, seemingly about to speak. Chavez-Smith cut him short.

"Give me the weapon. If you don't, I can have my bodyguards kill you and take it. Then where will you, or your group, be? You can trust me because I need you, just as you have needed me."

Herve seemed to think about that for a moment. In truth, he knew he had no option, but Chavez-Smith assumed he didn't wish to appear to give in so easily.

"Very well," Herve said finally, reaching into his pocket and taking out a small leather bag, which he handed to Chavez-Smith. The arms dealer took the bag, opened it and extracted a small plastic case. He opened it and revealed the chip.

"This is it," he breathed.

"All of this, just for that?" Herve mused. "It doesn't seem much, for so many lives."

Chavez-Smith smiled. It didn't reach as far as his eyes. "Gather the remainder of the cell and go to the château, then you will see."

"How long will you be?"

The arms dealer shrugged. "A day at most. We will cast off when you leave and berth at the next harbor. Then I will take this overland. It is important we lay a trail that will lead the opposition into nowhere."

"I understand," Herve agreed. Behind him, the cabin door opened, as though the arms dealer's bodyguard had been listening.

Herve left the room unnoticed by Chavez-Smith. The Chilean was still admiring the chip.

"THERE'S AN ARMED GUARD at the end," Bolan reported to the mercs as they sat in the tunnel leading out to the port. It emerged into the mouth of the docks, and ended in an iron grille—presumably easily maneuvered—that covered the storm drain and prevented it from being apparently accessible from the outside. The Executioner had made his way along to the final bend and taken a quick recon. The gendarmerie, although making no attempt to storm the tunnel, were keeping it under observation from cover.

"If they're at that end, then they'll sure as hell be at the other," Ross observed. "Question is, when do they get tired of waiting and come in after us?"

"When they have the plans of the complete underground and catacomb system," Bolan said promptly. "It's the early hours of the morning, and unless someone has these old blue-prints transferred to a computer, what are the chances of getting a local government officer out of bed to unlock an office, let alone search for a set of old plans that could be anywhere?"

Ross grinned. "If France is anything like England, less than zero."

Bolan nodded. "That's what we've got to hope for. Which means that we have a number of options to get out, the vast majority of which will be safe for the moment. We just need to find one, and then check it out before evac."

"Pity we can't just blast our way out, though. It would be quicker," Goldman pointed out.

"If you're going to stick with me, then you won't be doing that," Bolan said coldly. "Those guys out there have a difficult job, and they don't deserve to be shot down just because it could buy us time. They're not the enemy."

"All right. I know, I know," Goldman said, holding up his hands. "It was just an idea."

"A stupid one," Ross said pithily. "Come on, Cooper, where do we begin?"

Indicating for them to follow, Bolan led them back into the maze of tunnels, and back past the hollowed out chamber that housed the remains of the Destiny's Spear terrorists. They carried on into the dark, taking the route that Bolan had used to ambush the terrorists, groping their way through the blackness, using touch to find their way.

"This is it," the soldier said as his hands reached into empty air. "Can you feel that air current?"

"Yeah, and it's cooler than the air in here. Must lead outside," Ross said. "But where?"

"I figure that we'll come up about halfway between the docks and the harbor, which isn't ideal for being in a hurry, but will keep us away from the police."

"Sounds good to me. Lead on," the black mercenary answered.

The Executioner led the way down the pitch-black tunnel until a ray of illumination lit the shaft of an access tunnel, leading up to a manhole, the light coming through the holes in the grate from the streetlights above. Bolan jumped and caught the bottom rung of the rusty ladder, pulling himself up hand-over-hand until his feet were also on the rungs. From there, it was simple to clamber upward and lever the grate out of its socket.

The streetlights were reflecting on the windows of an apartment building. The manhole was on the sidewalk beside it. It was a quiet residential street, and there seemed to be no one to see them exit.

Relieved at this stroke of luck when everything had seemed to be going wrong, Bolan pulled himself out and then called down to Ross and Goldman, urging them to hurry. He kept watch while they lifted themselves out of the shaft, Goldman coming last and replacing the manhole cover.

Bolan slid the AKSU off his shoulder, disassembled it and stowed it on his combat harness. "Hardware away, gentlemen, and I'll have the Desert Eagle back," he added, taking the hand cannon from Goldman. Meanwhile, Ross stowed away the borrowed Beretta in its holster. He looked down at his rumpled and torn suit, and the ruined loafers, with distaste.

"Man, this is no way to earn a living. Look at the state of this suit. You wouldn't believe how much it cost me."

Bolan spared him an amused glance. "If that's all you're going to have to worry about before we're through, then things won't be that bad. Somehow, I have a feeling it's not going to go that way."

Without waiting for a response, the soldier jogged to the

end of the residential street and looked left and right along a road that was lined with shops, staring up at the street names to get his bearings.

"Jack, are you still with me?"

Silence. Bolan repeated the sentence. Still nothing. Somewhere along the way, the mike in the blacksuit had been damaged. He was on his own, with just Ross and Goldman for company and no backup from Grimaldi if they started to play their own game.

It wasn't a comforting thought.

10

Keeping to the side streets as much as possible, it took Mack Bolan and the two mercs almost a half an hour to negotiate the distance between their exit point and the harbor. There wasn't that much time to spare, but they were hampered by two things. First, the main streets of Marseilles were beginning to swarm with police, as the magnitude of the battle below in the catacombs began to come to light. Second, they were in no fit state to be seen by the police or any suspicious citizens. Bolan's shirt and pants were ripped and muddy, revealing the blacksuit and combat harness beneath. Ross's previously immaculate suit was ripped and torn, splattered in dirt and blood, and his loafers were barely hanging together. The only member of the trio who was able to blend into the background in any way was Goldman. His leather jacket was a little more scuffed and dirty than before, his jeans a little more ripped and muddy. But apart from the blood on his face where he had been hit, he looked more or less the same as ever, making him the one elected to go and recon the harbor when they reached port.

"You know where it is?" Bolan asked.

Goldman nodded. "Yeah, but are you sure you shouldn't go? You've actually been aboard Hector's yacht, and know a little more about the layout."

"We'll worry about that later," Bolan told him. "Your job is to check out the exterior security, assuming that the yacht is still there."

"And don't get caught or lose it again, Jimmy," Ross warned.

Goldman mimed surprise. "Me?"

Bolan felt a tension building in him as he and Ross watched the redheaded agent move away from their side alley cover and into the streetlights of the still crowded harbor area. There were increased police patrols, and the private security forces were more noticeable. Word of the disturbances in town had got back to the rich, and worried them, making them a little more paranoid.

The soldier felt frustrated at remaining in cover. He knew it was the easiest way to complete the recon, as Goldman could pass for one of the poorer sightseers who were now thronging the area, headed for the area where the gendarmes were staking out the entrance to the storm drain. But Bolan was still uneasy. He would have trusted Ross to do a good job, but Goldman was too much of a loose cannon, and too much a slave to his own short temper. Each moment that Goldman was away, the greater the danger of the whole thing blowing up in their faces.

Another thing that worried the Executioner was that he was still carrying the chemical weapons. He had hoped to call in Grimaldi and evac the weapons to the safety of the nearest U.S. air base before being shipped back to the States. They were well protected, but there was no denying that being on his person didn't exactly leave them in the safest place in the world.

Bolan didn't want the two mercenaries on the trail of the sonic chip alone, but he also didn't want to risk lives by carrying the chemical weapons and risking disaster. At the moment, he could see no way around this, and he would have to improvise if the chance arose.

He almost breathed a sigh of relief when he saw Goldman striding back toward them through the crowds. He wasn't being followed—he was even stopping to check—and his grim visage as he entered the alley told its own story.

"The yacht's gone," he said simply.

"You're sure?" Bolan queried. "You checked that it was the right berth?"

"I know you think I'm stupid, but I'm not," Goldman snapped. "I asked a few questions—discreetly—and it left over an hour ago. It's well out of port by now, and no one knew where it was headed, or even seemed interested. It's a complete dead end."

"Maybe, maybe not," Bolan mused. "If Chavez-Smith is making such a quick getaway, that suggests that he must have the chip."

"What good is that if we don't know where he's headed?" Goldman fumed.

"Maybe a lot," Bolan countered. "He has the chip, and he has to take it somewhere to strip it down and see how it works. That won't be at sea, that'll be inland. Which means he has to land and disembark somewhere. Now why wouldn't he just go by land in the first place?"

Ross grinned. "Because he wanted us to follow his damn boat, perhaps?"

Bolan nodded. "That's what I'd be thinking. And if that's the case, then we can forget about the boat and concentrate on our other lead."

"What other lead would that be?" Goldman said angrily.

Bolan resisted the temptation to deck the man. A brief glance at Ross told him that Goldman's partner felt much the same way. Instead, Bolan said calmly, "Signella sent someone out of the terrorist camp to deliver the chip. That someone knows where Chavez-Smith is headed. And I'll tell you another thing. From intel, I know that we met nowhere near the total of Destiny's Spear members back there. They're around this town, and I'd lay odds they'll be regrouping and moving out, maybe to wherever Chavez-Smith is headed."

Ross nodded. "So we track them down, maybe question them a little, and who knows?"

"Exactly. Okay, so we're not dressed for the part, but we need to get on this fast, or else we'll lose any initiative. They may already have gotten word to each other and be gone. I know you two did a lot of barhopping to find Signella in the first place, so I guess you know all the likely places."

"Yeah, and a lot of the likely suspects, as well," Ross replied, opting not to voice the question in his head as to how Bolan knew of their prior activities.

"Then we need to get moving. Hopefully, we won't look too conspicuous in some of these places," he added ruefully, looking down at his clothing, and that of Ross.

Goldman gave a short, harsh laugh. "Mate, compared to some of the people we're looking for, we look positively over-dressed."

THE FIRST TWO BARS yielded nothing, as they were deserted except for bar staff cleaning up the mess of the previous evening. Yes, they were open, but the incidents down at the docks and in the catacombs had cleared them out. In response to the question as to the best place to try next, each bar mentioned the other.

It was already beginning to look as though it was a dead end, but the third bar they visited had potential.

Ari's was run by a Greek who had jumped ship ten years before and settled in Marseilles. The basement drinking club could hardly even be dignified with the title bar, consisting of one room that had a makeshift bar cobbled together at the far wall, a counter hiding a fire ax, a baseball bat and an M-4000 shotgun that Ari kept on hand for difficult customers. The choice of liquor was limited to whatever Ari bought cheap that week from the sailors who stole it from cargoes or smuggled it in. And the ambience of the place would make a cockroach feel alienated.

"This is the place, I can feel it my bones," Goldman said with a savoring smile as he led them down the rickety iron stairs that led to the chipped and battered bar door.

"Cool it, Jimmy," Ross warned.

Bringing up the rear, Bolan could tell from the set of Goldman's body as he walked that this was a pointless statement.

Goldman kicked back the door so that it slammed against the wall with a resounding crash that cut through the low hum of conversation and the slightly louder jukebox, although to call the CD player and collection of disks by Ari's side a jukebox was dignifying it beyond need. The Greek's hand snaked beneath the counter, hovering over his choice of weapons.

"Easy, Ari, it was an accident," Goldman said, holding his hands up in a gesture of apology. "You know I'm heavy-handed, right? Remember me?"

"Yeah, the stupid bastard who knocked over one of my tables and annoyed my customers 'cause he can't hold his drink," the Greek growled in heavily accented French, remembering Ross and Goldman's previous visit, in search of Signella.

"That's me." Goldman shrugged. He walked up to the bar and reached out, faux-drunk, to embrace the Greek. "I'm sorry, mate," he sobbed, putting his arms around the bar owner.

The Greek was too startled to react, and so his hands stayed away from the weapons under the counter.

Guessing what was going down, Bolan hung back by the door, casually locking the toe of his boot around the timber, ready to close it. There was no stopping the redhead, so he might as well make sure the situation was secured.

The moment his arms were around the Greek, Goldman dropped the pretense, and slammed the startled barman onto the counter. It was a light wood, and Ari's face crashed into it. He screamed as splinters stuck in his nose and cheeks, before screwing up his eyes to try to protect them.

Bolan flicked the door with his foot, stepping away from the swing to allow it to slam shut. In the same motion he took the Beretta from its holster and arced it around the bar, making sure that the customers nearest the door had second thoughts about making an early exit. No one moved in the face of the 9 mm weapon.

Goldman let Ari go, and the Greek rose from the shattered surface of the bar with a snarl on his face. Before he had a chance to react, Goldman hit him, just once, but squarely between the eyes. The large silver ring that the redhead wore on the middle finger of his left hand ripped open the skin between the Greek's eyes, blood pouring down, obscuring his vision. He clattered backward into the shelves that stood to his rear, the few glasses and bottles falling into shards around his feet, and then his torso as he slumped down to join them. Goldman vaulted the bar and collected the weapons from underneath, slamming them on the top and picking up the M-4000. He racked a shell into the chamber.

"Y'know, sometimes I love my job." He smiled beatifically.

"Great, Jimmy. Now can we get on with the matter in hand?" Ross asked, his own Beretta drawn to cover the front of the bar.

Bolan looked around the room. There were sixteen patrons, clustered around three tables. One group of four—two men and two women. One of three—all men. The final table had eleven—five men and six women, probably the night's entertainment for the men, arranged around the long table that took up almost the whole left side of the room. He directed the Beretta and his first question to them.

"You heard about what happened earlier?"

"A lot of things happened earlier," one of the men stated. His hand was under the table, and Bolan saw the muscles in his forearm twitch.

One tap, and a line of 9 mm slugs bit into the table.

"Hands in plain sight. That goes for all of you," Bolan ordered.

The entire room placed their hands where they could be seen.

"I like it. They've got sense," Ross murmured.

"Exactly," Bolan returned. The emphasis had switched from Goldman to Bolan, and he had no intention of letting it slip. He wanted answers, quickly. "Let's cut the crap, people. You know what happened earlier. And now we want the rest of Destiny's Spear." Bolan scanned the faces. There were no terrorists that he could see, just a bunch of petty thieves and whores. "You may know where they are. There's still a lot of them out there."

"Why should we tell you?" questioned one of the women. "If we talk, then they will come and kill us. Perhaps worse."

"Lady, there's nothing worse that they could do to you," Goldman said with a sneer. "And if you don't talk, who says you'll get out of here alive anyway?" To emphasize his point, he fired a round into the ceiling of the bar with an explosive roar. Plaster rained down on them in the shocked silence that followed.

Bolan wasn't happy with the redhead's action. If anything, it would make these people clam up even more. And the M-4000 was not the most subtle of weapons. The noise alone was enough to alert outsiders to their presence.

"Excuse my colleague. He's a little rash," Ross said with a sidelong glance at Goldman. "But nonetheless, the point remains. You have to balance the possibility of surviving scumbags coming after you, against the very real threat of not getting out of here in one piece. So which, I wonder, is the option you will choose? The clock is ticking."

Bolan looked around the room. It was the men who looked the most nervous, either because they had nothing to tell and were afraid this would condemn them, or because they had a lot to tell and couldn't balance the odds. There was one in particular who seemed to be sweating. Bolan decided to go in for the kill.

"You," he snapped at the man, directing the barrel of the Beretta toward him. "Stand up."

The man did as he was told. He was about five foot six, skinny, with track marks down his arms, past the sleeves of his T-shirt, which hung off his emaciated frame. His sunken cheeks accentuated his bug eyes, which were staring nervously at the Beretta pointed in his direction. He ran a trembling hand through a shock of greasy, jet black hair.

"What do you know?" the Executioner asked softly. So softly, in fact, that it was far more menacing than if he had shouted the question.

"Nothing. What makes you think I do?" the man answered defensively. He looked around at the other inhabitants of the room defiantly, as though proving to them that he wouldn't succumb.

But this resolve was crumbled when Ari groaned and rose

groggily from his position on the floor behind the bar. He was halfway to his feet when, without looking, Goldman swung back with the stock of the M-4000, taking the Greek full in the face. His screams were muted by his own blood and broken teeth filling his mouth, and the back of his head cracked loudly against the wall. He sunk down again, unconscious.

This was enough for the nervous junkie.

"What do you want to know?"

"Where we can find the rest of Destiny's Spear. That's all," Bolan said calmly.

"Well, I'll tell you this much, you won't find them in Marseilles. Eh, maybe a couple, I dunno…"

"Talk sense," Bolan interjected.

The junkie paused. He appeared to be collecting his thoughts, and Bolan gave him a moment. Finally, he spoke.

"Okay, there's this guy Emil Herve, right? I buy junk from him sometimes. Anyway, I saw him tonight, only a couple of hours back, and I wanted to talk, but he told me he was in a hurry. Then I saw him go up to a couple of guys I know are Destiny Spear members. I'm not supposed to know, but I do, 'cause you hear things, right? I never figured him for one of them, but it was like he was giving out orders. And as soon as he left, they left. Like they were headed somewhere."

"And you happen to know where?" Bolan prompted.

The junkie shook his head. "No, I don't…and I'll swear to that, you can do what you want, but I don't. I do know where you can find Emil, though."

"That's more like it," Bolan said. "You tell me, and we'll leave everyone alone."

It still took the junkie a few seconds to muster the courage to give this last piece of information.

"A place called Nightmare, up at the eastern end of town.

He buys his junk there when he has a need, and by the look of him tonight, I figure he's gonna have a need. I heard him say something to one of the others about it when they were leaving. I was gonna go there and hit on him for some, later."

"Forget that idea," Bolan told him.

"You know the place?" he asked Ross and Goldman. Ross nodded. "Okay then, one more thing to do before we go. Jimmy, rip that phone out and find something you can fill with water," he ordered.

Goldman nodded and pulled the phone wire by the side of the counter out of the wall. He then found a battered ice bucket that he filled from a single cold tap by the filthy sink at the same side of the counter as the disconnected phone wire. He placed the full bucket on the counter and looked at the Executioner with a puzzled frown.

"Cell phones, people. Out on the tables with them, slowly. You are being covered," he reminded the patrons as they reached into pockets or purses to pull out phones.

When they were all on the tables, Bolan continued, "Errol, would you be so kind as to make sure no one can make any calls to warn anyone we're on our way?"

Ross grinned as the reason for the bucket full of water became clear. He turned and picked it off the bar, walking the length of the room and taking the phones, dropping them into the ice bucket so that they became saturated, excess water slopping onto the floor. When he had finished, he walked back and placed the full bucket on the bar.

"Right, move out. I'll cover you," Bolan said, opening the door and keeping the Beretta trained on the seated patrons while Ross and Goldman left, clattering up the iron stairs. Bolan followed, keeping the Beretta steady as he backed up the staircase to the sidewalk.

"Let's get after this Emil guy before it's too late. I figure you know what he looks like?"

"Yeah, we've seen him—and know all about him," Goldman replied. "This is going to be a pleasure."

11

The first gray light of dawn was beginning to creep into the sky above the neon haze of Marseilles as the three men made their way toward the docks. Goldman had complained when Bolan insisted that they return to the harbor to collect his car before driving to the outskirts of town to the Nightmare club where they hoped to pick up the trail of Destiny's Spear. But although the town wasn't large, the trail was almost cold, and they needed to get to the club quickly. This was why the volatile Goldman had objected to them returning to the harbor, in the opposite direction. But if they had the car, then the journey would be cut by half, and less dangerous in terms of being spotted. As morning broke, Bolan was aware that the streets would be teeming with gendarmerie looking for anyone as obviously ragged as they were. To keep some kind of cover was an imperative.

Ross and Bolan waited once more in an alley while Goldman walked down to the harbor area with Bolan's car keys. Still the least conspicuous, it was up to him to retrieve the Citroën.

There was another reason that the Executioner wanted the car. In the trunk he still had his combat bag, with enough hardware to start a small war. He didn't want that to fall into the hands of a car thief, or the gendarmerie. If the latter found it, then the Sûreté would become involved, the weapons could possibly be traced to the U.S. Air Force, and things could get out of hand. Better to retrieve it now.

It was still an anxious wait until Goldman appeared at the wheel of the car, a few minutes later. Bolan hadn't told either of the mercenaries about the hardware stowed in the trunk, and had no intention of doing so unless it was either relevant or necessary. The less they knew about that, the better.

"Well, I've got your car, so can we get going now?" Goldman asked impatiently as he pulled up at the mouth of the alley.

"You drive," Bolan said as he slid into the passenger seat, Ross taking the rear. "Believe me, Jimmy, this will be quicker in the long run. And it means we have transport if we draw another blank and have to chase leads."

"I suppose," Goldman grumbled. He ground the gears in anger and set off toward the outskirts of town. It was obvious that he knew where he was headed, so Bolan didn't bother to question him. Instead, the Executioner pondered a few thoughts of his own.

If Chavez-Smith was laying a false trail with his yacht and was headed inland, where would he be going? It would be somewhere secluded, probably outside of a small village or town rather than inside. And it would have to be a fairly large spread if he intended to gather the remaining terrorists to him. Just to house them would entail a large house or outbuilding. Good security was another must. Someone with the Chilean's experience wouldn't skimp on this.

So the kind of place they were looking for was easy to

guess, not so easy was the location. It could be anywhere. If they couldn't pick up any of the terrorists who were straggling, then he hoped that they could at least pick up an overheard clue.

Bolan's other problem was the faulty mike on the blacksuit. Contact with Grimaldi had been vital to his game plan. Having the pilot as backup, and ready for evac, was integral to the success of his operation. This was going to be too big to go into alone. He had the mercs with him, but theirs was an uneasy alliance, and could fall apart when the microchip was in their grasp. Grimaldi would know that Bolan had been busy, as he would have switched to monitoring local news and police broadcasts. It wouldn't take much for the pilot to guess who was behind the war in the catacombs. But Bolan needed to check in with Grimaldi and brief him, and also to get a replacement mike. Anything else would be exposing himself to unnecessary risks—and they were the ones he would always try to avoid.

When they had some intel, he would have to take the mercs with him to the airfield. Although he was loathe to let them know the strength of his resources, it was possible that the knowledge could make them think twice about doublecrossing him.

All told, the situation was more of a snafu than usual. But the time to really worry about this would be later. First, they had to deal with finding Emil Herve. Bolan knew nothing else about him, whereas Ross and Goldman knew who he was. As they drew up outside the club Nightmare, Bolan wished they would share some information with him. But his questions had been met with noncommittal answers. They wanted to assert themselves. Let them, for now, Bolan thought.

"Lovely looking little shit house, this, isn't it?" Goldman

said as they crossed the street to a three-story building with blacked-out windows. A small sign, lit in red and blue neon, named the club, and there was no sound from within.

"I could have put it with more finesse," Ross commented, "but the point remains, I guess."

"It looks closed," Bolan pointed out, ignoring them.

"Looks being the operative word," Ross answered, taking note of the Executioner for the first time since they had regained the car. "It always looks like this, and it's a 24/7 kind of place. If Emil Herve isn't here, then there's going to be someone who knows where he's gone."

Goldman strode up to the front door that stood beneath the neon sign. He pressed the intercom buzzer and waited for a tinny voice to answer: *"Oui?"*

"Tell Jojo the boys are back in town," Goldman said in his appalling French.

The door clicked and Goldman pushed it open. "Very exclusive," he said over his shoulder as he entered. "They change the password every three days, and we were screwed if this was day four."

There was something in the redhead's tone that told the soldier this was going to be messy, so he brought out the Desert Eagle, inserting a fresh clip. He wasn't planning on doing a lot of shooting at this stage, and knew that the hand cannon was a good deterrent to potential enemies just by sight alone.

"Good idea," Ross murmured, unleathering his Beretta.

Goldman was taking the stairs to the first floor two at a time, and Bolan hung back a couple of steps. If the redhead ran straight into trouble, the soldier wanted a few feet of space in which to move.

"Ground floor?" Bolan whispered over his shoulder.

"Not in use. All of the action is up these stairs," Ross replied, grasping the reasoning.

At the top of the stairs was another closed door. The distant sounds of music could be heard, and the low hum of some conversation, but it was the slowed-down, lazy sound of early-morning wind-downs. Chances were that the staff and customers were too drunk or stoned to react.

Goldman reached the top of the stairs and kicked open the door leading into the club room. It cannoned back into the wall and he marched across to where the DJ was still spinning a few tunes. Felling him with one sharp jab to his gaping and surprised jaw, Goldman then shut off the music. The low hum died out in astonishment.

"Heads up, people, I've got a few questions I'd like to ask all of you."

"Police?" asked the tattooed man behind the bar, his hand sliding out of sight.

"No, which is why I'll have no hesitation in blowing you away if you don't put your hands back on the counter," Bolan replied as he entered the room. The Desert Eagle was enough for the barman to put his hands back.

"And we'll have a little light, please," Goldman snapped. "I know you think daylight is your enemy, but I want to see what you're all doing."

"And that'll be about now, thank you," Ross said to the security man, who'd had a sudden change of career in mind after seeing Bolan's Desert Eagle, and was about to make a run for the stairs when Ross appeared in the doorway to block his flight.

Hands lifted in a gesture of surrender, the security man backed away to a small black box mounted on the wall. Carefully—his eyes fixed on the Beretta—he flipped open the box and turned up the lighting until it was painfully bright in the club.

Looking around, Bolan felt that the Nightmare was aptly named. The room was small, with a well-stocked bar. There were booths around the dance floor, which was littered with broken glass and the detritus of a heavy evening. Obviously, at one point the place had been busy, but now there were only the last stragglers, about twenty people, half and half male and female. Some were almost comatose, some were still awake and others were bright-eyed and overly twitchy in a way that suggested just a little too much coke or speed. The barman and the security man made twenty-two in all. The DJ didn't count, as he was still unconscious.

"Now then, I'd like you all to stand in the middle of the floor there, where we can see you all clearly," Goldman said with a smile. He was relishing this, and Bolan had that uneasy feeling again. If they eventually traced the Chilean and the terrorists, Bolan had the feeling that he may have to spend more time worrying about Goldman than about the real enemy. But Bolan needed his help to find the sonic weapon, so he'd put up with his outrageous behavior for a little longer.

Slowly, gathering themselves, the people moved out of the booths and onto the brightly lit dance floor, the livelier ones supporting those who were virtually unable to move under their own energy. The barman and security man joined them.

Bolan looked at them, and had an uneasy feeling. He didn't hold out much hope of getting anything approaching sense from these people. But that wasn't what was prickling at him. There was something else. This was too simple. There was an angle that wasn't being covered…

From the corner of his eye, he had caught the faintest movement behind the bar. There was a door that led into a storeroom, or perhaps a staircase to the upper level. Wherever it led, it was occupied. Someone was concealed there, and now they were moving the door.

Someone hiding wouldn't want that door to budge. They would only be moving it if they were on the offensive.

Bolan swung his arm and around and loosed off three rounds from the Desert Eagle. The roar of the .44 Magnum pistol in the quiet room was deafening, his finger squeezing the trigger smoothly and rapidly so that the three slugs seemed to run into one. The door splintered under the impact, the black-painted wood suddenly spangled with white wood stars from beneath the paint job. It was a light wood, and no obstacle to the heavy Magnum slugs.

The door swung open under the deadweight it now concealed. A man, heavyset and in his late thirties, fell forward and hit the floor behind the bar. He was dead, three large holes in his chest and stomach testifying to how little the wood of the door had acted as a defense. He was still clutching a crudely sawed-off shotgun.

As the echo of the Desert Eagle died away, Bolan was aware of the screams from some of the women—and some of the men—on the dance floor. He turned back to them.

"Quiet!" he yelled. "You have nothing to fear as long as you cooperate."

The note of authority in his voice seemed to calm the crowd, and only a few were still looking over toward the bar. The rest of them were looking at either Bolan or Ross. They ignored Goldman, who had no gun in his hand, but they turned at the sound of his voice, having almost forgotten him.

"Right, now, just looking over you lot of filth, I can see that the particular piece of scum that I'm after isn't here. So maybe one of you would be kind enough to tell me where I can find Emil Herve."

There was a tight-lipped silence.

"What did the man say? Nothing to fear as long as you co-operate. Only you're not, are you? And that really is too bad. Because I'd say, looking at you, none of you have really got the balls to be quiet. So I reckon—"

Bolan was getting tired of the way in which the redhead seemed to be getting off on the situation. "Jimmy, Errol, do you recognize any of these people?" he snapped, cutting off Goldman.

"No. No Destiny's Spear among them," Ross replied calmly, eyes flitting from Goldman to Bolan and back again. He could sense the tension coming from the soldier, and also knew that his partner was oblivious to it.

"Cooper, you really should let me handle these people my way," Goldman said wearily. "We haven't got time to piss about. This lot couldn't be terrorists in a million years. They've gone, but I bet this group buy half their drugs off them, and don't mind listening in to a few conversations they're not supposed to. I bet they know exactly where Herve and his terrorist friends have gone."

While he was speaking, Goldman moved down from the DJ booth, across the dance floor to where the customers were gathered. Suddenly, he seized one of the bright-eyed, spaced-out young men and pulled him toward him, taking the Smith & Wesson pistol from his pocket and holding it to the man's head. In the bright lights of the room, Bolan could see a dark patch spread on the front of the man's tight black jeans where he urinated in fear. Goldman held the gun to his temple.

"I bet a coked-up speed freak like you listens in, eh? I bet you could tell me where they'd gone, no problem."

"N-n-n-no," his captive stammered, the word barely escaping his lips.

"Let him go," Bolan said coldly, shifting his aim with the Desert Eagle so that it was focused on the redhead.

"Aw, you've got to be kidding," Goldman said, shifting so that his captive formed a shield.

"I could blow your head off from here," Bolan said quietly. "If these people aren't connected to Destiny's Spear, then we have no need to harm them."

"He says, after blowing away that geezer behind the door," Goldman spit.

"That was different," Bolan said in a level tone. "He was a threat. They aren't. Put the gun down. Now."

There was a moment where he thought he would have to fire. Goldman's eyes fixed on his, and Bolan's finger tightened on the trigger, squeezing gently.

"Okay, okay, have it your way," Goldman said, disgusted, as he stepped back, holding the gun muzzle upward and pushing the man back into the clustered group.

"That's better.' Bolan turned his attention to the people and addressed them. "You know what we want, and you know that he's barely in control. Next time I may not be able to stop him. So perhaps you'd better speak now, so we can leave."

He didn't know if it would work. He was counting on their collective lack of nerve. It was a good call. An anorexically thin woman in a long black dress and white face makeup, who was comforting Goldman's victim, looked up.

"If I tell you something, you will go, yes?" Her French was halting, and Bolan pinned down her accent as Spanish.

"If it is of use," he said simply.

"I know this man you seek," she said in reply. "Yes, we buy from him. He is a slimy, boastful piece of shit, and he has a favorite woman who works here. A whore. Who else would have him?"

She paused, as though expecting an answer. It struck the soldier as odd that a junkie would be so judgmental, but he held his tongue, waiting for her to continue.

"You will not find her here now, as she went with him, but he was boasting to her about the mansion he would take her to in Provence, somewhere near Aix. He wanted it to be a surprise, but he couldn't help letting that slip. He said it had extensive vineyards."

Bolan allowed himself a small smile. His guess about the type of location had been correct.

"Anyone else hear anything?" he said. There were murmurs from the group, but nothing of any importance. Directing his attention to the Spanish woman, he asked, "Did you see them leave?"

She shook her head, but added, "It cannot have been that long ago, less than an hour since he took the last of our money."

Bolan nodded. "Okay. That's all we need to know. Now, my colleagues and I are going to leave. Slowly. I would suggest you wait there for five minutes and do nothing."

But from the look of the dejected group, there was nothing to cause concern. He waved the Desert Eagle at Goldman, who skirted the group and headed for the stairs. Bolan then began to withdraw, mindful of the fact that Goldman had the car keys, and the last thing he wanted was to be left holding the backline while Ross and Goldman sped off. He backed past Ross, who looked momentarily confused, then automatically followed.

As they left the building, in the early morning light, Bolan kept a watch even though he was sure they had nothing to fear.

Goldman fired up the car and pulled away. "Well, I thought that went well," the redhead said in a satisfied voice.

His words astounded the Executioner, who was more than ever convinced Goldman was more of a threat than an asset.

12

"The thing is, just where exactly do we start?" Goldman asked as he piloted the Citroën out of the early-morning Marseilles traffic and onto the freeway. "I mean, we know it's a big place near Aix, but that still covers a hell of a lot of ground, and we don't have a lot of time."

"You know more about the stolen goods than I do. What's your estimation?" Bolan asked, before adding, "and bear in mind that the Chilean's customer is Mehmet Attaturk. His patience isn't what you could call one of his virtues."

"You know this for sure?" Ross queried.

Bolan nodded. "He was on the yacht, and nothing's going to bring him out of even partial cover unless it's important. This chip is."

Ross bit his lip and considered an answer before saying, "Look, they didn't tell us that much, but this is pretty advanced engineering and programming that we're talking about. In order to get it back to the engineer and get a viable result from taking the damn thing apart, we've got to be looking at a couple of days."

"What if he's just going to give him the damn thing and not bother about taking it apart?" Goldman interjected as he overtook a vehicle on the inside lane, leaving a protesting Volvo driver in his wake.

"Slow down, Jimmy. We don't even know exactly where we're headed yet," Ross yelled. "Keep it together, for God's sake."

"Chavez-Smith would try to buy time to take it apart," Bolan stated. "If he has that secret, then he has more money and power—more than he's ever seen—in one little package. He's not the type to turn that down." The soldier shook his head. "No, I figure he can buy a little time by claiming he had to detour to shake us off, and that'll be when his people get to work on the chip. The other thing is this, if he doesn't have anything other than off-loading the chip on his mind, then why gather the rest of Destiny's Spear?"

"You figure he could be planning some kind of test?" Ross asked quietly.

"Intel reports show that he has sympathies with their goals, and wasn't merely using them as a cover or a private army," Bolan replied. "Put their numbers together with a weapon like that, and the links they have with other neo-fascist organizations in Europe, the UK and Ireland, and in the States, and all of a sudden it looks a little different."

"You're clouding the issue," Goldman snapped. "Our job is to get the chip back. You shouldn't even be here. Anything that Chilean has planned for his tin soldiers has nothing to do with us."

"It does," Bolan said coldly, "because the people who hired you are still part of the U.S. military and administration, even if they are working contra to the Oval Office. You think they'd want their little secret getting disseminated like that? We're coming from different places, but our aim has become the same."

"I don't buy it."

"How are you going to find Chavez-Smith quickly? There's a very narrow window in which to achieve the objective, and you don't know where to start. You're going to be wandering blind—"

"And you're not?" Goldman sneered.

"I have backup that can help identify possible targets. If we use that, we can find them. If not, we'll probably miss that chance."

"You have 'backup'? Who'll shoot us down as soon as they see us, right?" Goldman asked, taking his eyes off the road as he passed a swerving, unsteady truck that looked as though it was many years past its roadworthiness.

Bolan glanced at the surrounding scenery and the road sign that flashed past. He had to convince Goldman quickly, or they would be past the turnoff for the airfield.

"I have a backup who responds to my orders. And I give you my word. You're an irritating jackass, and I could have eliminated you at any time during the past few hours. But I didn't, because we need each other's knowledge right now, like it or not. It's only by working together that we stand a chance of getting that chip back before the Chilean knows its secrets, and it's sold to Attaturk. And with the situation as it is…"

Ross spoke from the back seat. He had been silent for some time, considering Bolan's words.

"Jimmy, whatever you think about Cooper, he's right. Cooper, you know there'll come a point where we'll have a conflict of interest, and then it's going to get nasty. But right now we do need a marriage of convenience. You have my word—if you think it's worth anything—that we'll follow your lead on this."

Goldman was livid. "Errol, how stupid are you? We're walking into a trap."

Ross shook his head. "I don't think so. Not at this point. We still need each other too much. Besides, where was this backup when we were in the town?"

"A communication breakdown. Which we need to get remedied, as well as picking up as much information as we can."

Goldman suddenly pulled the car onto a hard shoulder. "So can you two, if you've settled what the hell it is that we're doing—not that my opinion counts for much, I know—tell me where the hell I'm supposed to be headed?"

"Considering you've been driving blindly since we left the Nightmare, I thought you had some kind of supernatural insight," Ross said with a bland sarcasm. "Now calm down, Jimmy. We need to be businesslike on this one."

Bolan allowed himself a smile. "I'm glad you see it that way. Jimmy, take the next turnoff and double back a couple of kilometers. There's a turnoff for an airfield that we need to take. My backup is waiting there, and we can get cleaned up and refitted while we try to pin down the target location... and I mean all of us," he emphasized.

Goldman grunted and swung the car onto the freeway again. His silence was the most eloquent thing to come from him for some time. The soldier breathed a sigh of relief. If Ross could keep Goldman under control, and Grimaldi could locate the château or farm where the Chilean had retreated, then it was possible they could clear up this mess.

"SIR, THE CITROËN with Colonel Stone has just entered the airfield perimeter."

Jack Grimaldi snapped out of the reverie into which he had sunk. Since the news and police band reports on the events in the catacombs under Marseilles had abated, there had been reports of two separate incidents in drinking clubs that had ended with one man dead and several injuries. Each time three men had been involved.

One of the descriptions sounded like Bolan, all right, but what worried Grimaldi was that the other two had fitted the descriptions of Ross and Goldman. The pilot felt uneasy about any alliances that Bolan had formed with these guys. He had more information on them now that Kurtzman had managed to get past the fire walls that had prevented him getting full file access, and the team at Stony Man had hacked into places that weren't even supposed to exist.

After so many missions together Grimaldi knew Bolan probably better than just about anyone else, and if he was allying himself with these guys, there was a good reason. If only the mike on the blacksuit hadn't been damaged along the way, he'd have been able to keep contact.

"Sir, did you catch that?" Walters asked hesitantly when Grimaldi didn't immediately respond.

"Yeah. Thanks, Walters. Is he on his own?"

"No, sir, the sentry I posted reports two other men. Colonel Stone is not driving. They match..." He indicated the printouts Grimaldi had in front of him.

"Yeah, I kind of figured they would. Okay, here's what we're going to do. We're going to give them a cautious but friendly welcome. We can assume that the Colonel is allied with them, but we keep a few incentives on hand in case it gets rough, okay?"

"Understood, sir," Walters said. He unholstered his Walther P-38 and checked it. "I haven't had to fire one of these for a few years, sir, so I may be a little rusty."

"Anyone who can tell me that probably won't be," Grimaldi said with a grin as he checked his H&K MP-5 before concealing it beneath the flight jacket he was still wearing. "Let's go for it."

The two men walked out into the morning air to greet the vehicle as it approached the control tower and the surrounding bunkers. The light breeze brought a crispness to the air that wakened Grimaldi totally, so that every little thing around seemed sharpened. The early-morning sun was still low, and caught on the windshield of the car so that he was unable to see clearly inside. He and Walters walked a few paces across the grass and then waited, the USAF officer moving away from Grimaldi to make a cluster shot from the car impossible. It was a precaution—one Grimaldi hoped they wouldn't need.

The car rolled to a halt. The normal traffic of the airfield had already begun, and although it was quiet, there were planes preparing to take off, with a few engineers and pilots wandering the airfield. No other cars had taken this route, sticking to the roads leading to the parking lot and the hangars. If ever they wanted to be noticed, this was the way to do it, which would make a confrontation awkward. As with all of Bolan's missions, it was important to keep as much of a low profile as possible.

Three doors opened on the car simultaneously, and all three occupants exited the vehicle. Grimaldi was able to identify Ross and Goldman immediately. They stood away, their hands free.

Bolan took a step forward. "It's okay, Jack. We've got a major problem on our hands, too much to worry about petty divisions right now."

Grimaldi breathed a sigh of relief but still didn't relax. From the corner of his eye, he could see that Walters was still poised.

Bolan reached under the torn shirt and produced the package containing the chemical weapons, which he held out to the USAF officer.

"Mission accomplished. At least, the official one. These are the stolen flasks containing chemical weapons, Walters. Take them and get them shipped back to your base."

Walters came forward and took the package gingerly. "I'll get on it right away, Colonel."

"You do that," Bolan said, turning back to Grimaldi. He indicated the two mercenaries standing behind him. "We've lost Chavez-Smith and the sonic weapon they're after. I'm going after it with them. We need to get cleaned up, reequipped, and I need to know if you have maps and references for the Aix area."

"Not on paper, but I can tap into any information on-line," Grimaldi answered. "What do you mean, you're going with them and they're getting reequipped?"

"Exactly what I say, Jack," Bolan replied, leading Grimaldi toward the cinder-block bunker that was his base. "Chavez-Smith has at least twenty men surrounding him, and we need a little help."

Grimaldi looked over his shoulder to see Ross and Goldman follow at a distance. "Maybe you should wait until you see the intel Aaron finally managed to get on these guys."

"I doubt if it'll change my mind," Bolan replied, "but it might help me keep them in check, especially the redhead. He's too hotheaded for his own good."

BOLAN SENT Ross and Goldman to shower and change under the auspices of Walters. There was a shower room for the use of the airfield's clients, and members of the flying club that used the facilities, and Walters had made sure that these were secured for the use of the solider and his associates. There was a subtle presence around the airfield that Bolan's trained eye had spotted, but which was otherwise unobtrusive. The Executioner was impressed with the young USAF officer.

Bolan wanted them out of the way while he discussed matters with Grimaldi, and that was the best way to do it. He noticed the glances that passed between the mercs when he made the suggestion, but knew that he was in the driving seat at this point.

"Sarge, those guys are nothing but trouble," Grimaldi began as Bolan walked to the Citroën as soon as Ross and Goldman were out of sight. "Aaron's report on them shows that they're responsible for at least twelve missions on behalf of hostile agencies that have ended in the deaths of several civilians. Those bastards don't care who they hit."

"I know, Jack, I know," Bolan replied as he took the combat bag from the trunk. "That's why I didn't let them know what I had stashed in the trunk. Goldman is the real problem. He's out of control. Ross would be a good soldier on his own, but he seems to spend half his time keeping the other one in check. I can't work out why he stays with him."

"Loyalty, Sarge. The biggest tie there is," Grimaldi added, knowing Bolan of all people would understand the import of his words. "Goldman saved Ross's life when they were working as special branch officers for British intelligence."

Grimaldi shrugged. "Anyway, Ross figures he owes Goldman, and they're efficient enough. They get results."

"Which is why I don't want to be up against them until the end, Jack. The Chilean has a small army at his location. I need the four of us against them. As for what happens when we get the chip back, well, we'll have to see."

"A chip? That's all it is?" Grimaldi asked in astonishment as he jogged alongside Bolan back to the cinderblock bunker. "That's going to be like a needle in a haystack."

"Not if Hector is in the middle of taking the chip apart to see how it works."

As they entered the blockhouse, and Bolan unpacked and double-checked the contents of the combat bag, he filled Grimaldi in on all that he had learned about the sonic weapon, and the suppositions on which they were currently working. When he had finished, Grimaldi nodded grimly.

"It doesn't give us a lot of time, that's for sure. I'll check in with Stony Man and see if they can come up with any intel on Attaturk's employers and their agents. The Turk may not be going to pick up that chip alone, in which case we want to know the strength of his forces. And I'll see if any of the other terrorist groups in this part of the world have made any arrangements with Destiny's Spear. That could give us a clue to location."

Bolan grinned. "It amazes me that they think the Internet

is safe to broadcast their movements on. Guess it's a good job their cyphers are no match for Kurtzman. The other thing you could get them working on is any real estate bought and sold in the past twelve months around Aix that could be of a relevant size. We can check local maps, but if they can tap in and get recent transactions, we can cross-reference. Chavez-Smith's files showed nothing, right?" When Grimaldi nodded, Bolan continued, "He would have purchased under a cover name, but I can't imagine too many sizeable properties in that region have changed hands lately."

Bolan stripped off the ragged shirt and the ripped pants, then removed the weaponry on the combat harness. He detached the broken mike. "I'll need a replacement for this," he said. "Get Walters on it."

"Okay, Sarge. Meantime, I'll get the Farm onto our little problem and see what I can call up for the Aix region. It'll be good to get out of here and out in the field again. I need fresh air."

Bolan clapped him on the shoulder. "I figure that by the time we've finished with this, we would have had more than enough...if we get out in one piece."

"It's those risks that make it worthwhile, right?" Grimaldi said without looking around from the monitor.

Bolan left him to his task and exited the bunker to go and take a shower. He knew that the water would freshen him up, and although he could have done with a couple of hours sleep to replenish, he doubted if they would have the time before they had to move out.

The soldier jogged across the field to the building housing the showers, feeling the warming morning sun. The sky was dappled with low cumulus clouds, and the azure blue beyond was almost magical. Days like this, days for people to be free and not live in fear.

This thought spurred him on, and by the time he reached the showers, he was ready to forgo sleep and keep running.

The finish line had come in sight, but there were still a lot of hurdles to clear.

13

Bolan returned from the showers to find Walters waiting for him, along with Ross and Goldman. Both were dressed in combat fatigues that fit, but only just. Goldman didn't seem to mind, but Bolan was amused to note that the fastidious Ross looked distinctly uncomfortable.

"Sorry that the USAF doesn't have made-to-measure tailoring," he couldn't resist remarking.

Ross had the good grace to look abashed. "Yeah, well, it's the best under the circumstances, right?"

Bolan turned his attention to Grimaldi. The note of humor died in his throat as he caught sight of the pilot's stony visage.

"Problems?"

Grimaldi screwed his face into an expression of distaste and disgust. "Something like that. You wouldn't believe the amount of real estate that's been sold and resold around the Aix region in the past few years. It's going to take some time to unravel it all and try to narrow down the field."

Bolan shook his head in amazement. "You wouldn't think that such an isolated region would be so popular," he stated as he took in some of the information displayed on screen. Grimaldi had also printed some of the lists to cross-reference by hand.

"Blame it on us Brits," Ross said with a shrug. Bolan gave a questioning glance, and the merc continued, "Few years back there was a bestseller in England, and a TV series from it. Seems some journalist had taken off to Provence for a year to chill out, and then wrote a book about how wonderful it was. England's not hot, not pretty and not laid-back…at least, not where most people have to live. So they bought into the dream, and there you are—lots of Brits buying property and then trying to off-load it when they find out it's not as wonderful as they thought it would be."

"Yeah, I can see that," Grimaldi said, casting an eye over the lists in front of him. "A lot of these are English names."

"Think we could cut a corner and discard them?" Bolan queried. "Do we know if the Chilean ever uses English cover names?"

"Wait…" Grimaldi cleared the screen and then brought up the file on Chavez-Smith downloaded to him by Aaron Kurtzman. Over his shoulder, Bolan read the information on display.

Hector Chavez-Smith was all-too fond of using English cover names. The fact that his own name was double-barreled in Spanish and English was no affectation. Like many Chileans, his name was a reflection of the two colonial powers that had used Chile for farming at the turn of the twentieth century.

Which was absolutely no help at all to Bolan and Grimaldi.

"Dammit, we're just going to have to find another way of sifting the information," Bolan said.

Grimaldi sat back in his chair and tapped his teeth with the end of a pen, his mind racing to try to find a way of organizing the task. He wanted to locate the Chilean just as swiftly as the soldier.

"How about this. We've got the maps of the Aix area. Cross-reference those with any property over a certain size to rule out the places that just aren't big enough for the kind of personnel we know he has, then cross-reference again with those that have changed hands within, say, an eighteen-month window."

"Why eighteen months?" Ross asked. He and Goldman had kept out of the discussion so far, but had been listening intently.

"Because we know from his file that Chavez-Smith had no property—under any name at all—in this area at that time. That was the last full security sweep on him, about the time of the Oval Office intervention on the Irish Peace Talks," Grimaldi answered.

"Yeah, I remember that all right," Bolan said wryly, recalling the concern that the Chilean was selling direct to splinter groups on both sides of the divide.

"So anything between then and now, of the right size, in the area…that could be it?" Ross asked.

"Yeah. Of course, we have to do some recons if there's more than one," Grimaldi mused, "which, knowing the way things have run so far on this one, is not exactly unlikely."

"So where do we get started?" Bolan asked, picking up a handful of printouts and looking at the screen.

"We don't start at all. At least, you don't," Grimaldi stated, taking the pile of paper from Bolan's hands. "I think me and Walters can do this, right?" he asked of the officer.

Walters nodded. "Absolutely, sir. No problem at all."

"And you," Grimaldi continued, poking Bolan in the chest with his forefinger, "should get some rest. And that goes for those guys, too," he added, directing a thumb at Ross and Goldman. "We've been sitting here waiting, whereas you've all been in a heavy-duty combat situation. If we're going to pull this one out of the bag, then you need to be fresh. Go and get a couple of hours' shut-eye if you can. You're so wired that you'll be more of a pain than a help at the moment, okay?"

"Yeah, maybe you're right about that," Bolan told himself. "Can you fix us up with somewhere to sleep?" he asked Walters.

"I've got some men on the clubhouse, keeping it secured. We can make up some beds there."

"As long as it doesn't take too long," Bolan reiterated to Grimaldi. "We need to move quickly on this."

"I know.' Grimaldi nodded. "But I can't make any promises on this. One thing, though, the longer you keep hassling me, the longer it'll take me to get started."

THE EXECUTIONER WOKE suddenly from a dreamless sleep. He was never far from the surface of consciousness, and the creak of the door and the soft footfalls of someone stepping into the room pulled him back to life.

Frank Walters was standing by the door, which was open only enough to reveal that it was twilight outside.

"What is it?" Bolan asked, his eyes adjusting to the gloom. "My God, how long have we been sleeping?"

"About twelve hours, sir," Walters replied.

"How long? Why didn't—"

"There was no point in waking you until now, sir, because we were making very little progress. This Chavez-Smith is one hell of a slick operator. We've been back and forth over those maps and real-estate transactions, and we couldn't get the list down below a dozen."

"Twelve… That'll take a hell of a lot of time to recon," Bolan said, almost to himself.

"It would have been pointless, as well," Walters stated. "Seems that he's too wily to do anything as simple as buy."

Bolan's brow furrowed. "What do you mean?"

"We've also been monitoring police-band broadcasts and news agencies for unusual events in the area. It figures that if there are that many people moving into an isolated spot, or there are any tests or accidents, then word will get out."

"And it has, right?"

Walters allowed the ghost of a smile to cross his lips. "You could say that. Something very odd is happening up near Aix. In a small village called Santon. It seems that no one can contact anyone there. And I mean anyone. It still has a manual telephone exchange, and that's out. The local gendarmerie are out. The fire department is out. The doctor is out. People with relatives are starting to complain that they can't contact them. All this over the space of a day, but it's building up to a hell of a lot of clamor."

"And let me guess—anyone who's tried to get in has suddenly gone out of touch, right?"

"Exactly," Walters answered. "Cell phones seem to have entered some region where their signals can't reach, even though there was no sign of this yesterday or the day before."

Bolan was now on his feet and pulling on his pants. "Get Ross and Goldman. We need to get fully briefed right now. Have you got that blacksuit with a replacement mike?"

"Ready and waiting, Colonel. I'll make sure the others are ready."

Walters left Bolan to finish dressing. Thoughts were racing through Bolan's head. The fact that there was such a sudden and large blind spot around a village near Aix had to mean something, especially when the weapon in the Chilean's possession had the capability to transfix and immobilize people so easily.

Bolan left the room and crossed from the clubhouse to the cinder-block bunker where Grimaldi had been working. The evening air was cool and fresh. He could hear Ross and Gold-man coming up behind him, in heated discussion. Goldman was complaining to Ross that their room—Walters had made sure that two rooms were prepared, so that Bolan could sleep alone—had been guarded, like they weren't trusted. He was amused to hear Ross point out that it was only natural that they be under guard.

Ross, he could work with easily, but there was still that nagging feeling about Goldman. Bolan dismissed the thought as he entered the blockhouse to find Walters waiting with Grimaldi.

"So what have you got for me?" he asked without preamble.

"Would you believe that the sly bastard hasn't bought any property around Aix at all?" Grimaldi said with a mix of weari-ness and astonishment. "Hours spent referencing and cross-referencing, and I'd lay everything on this being the answer."

"This being?" Bolan queried.

"This being the events Frank has just told you about. Sus-picious enough, but I had another look over the maps of the area, and also the real estate thereabouts. There's a château with a vineyard that's a good size for Chavez-Smith's base of op-erations, but it's something that we wouldn't have considered."

"The reason?" Bolan knew Grimaldi's exasperated pause was because he wanted Bolan to ask.

"Because it hasn't changed hands for at least two hundred years. It's been owned by the same family for that time. But—and here's where he was smart—he didn't bother buy-ing it. He rented it. That way it doesn't show up on transac-tions for real estate. I had to spend half an hour getting hold of the local real estate management company on the phone, and then threatening them with anything I could think of to get them to admit that it was being rented. Apparently the family hit financial problems about a year ago, and an old family friend called David Martin—a nice, English kind of name—came in with a proposition. He would rent it in return for being able to occupy it without interference. He's a reclusive art dealer, allegedly."

"With a South American accent, no doubt. I wonder if they really did need the money, or if he just leaned on them a little?"

"If it's all aboveboard with rent and a management company, no one locally is going to talk about, or snoop into, the new occupants."

Bolan shook his head. "He knew anyone going after the chip wouldn't think of him renting. But with enough pressure on whoever…"

"So, he has no on-site landlord, and nothing obvious to tie to the property."

"Looks like we couldn't have found him until he started using that sonic weapon." He turned to Ross and Goldman. "You were briefed on the weapon, right? I know it was a strictly need-to-know basis, but they must have given you some indication of the effects. Does it last after the weapon is in use, or is he still using it if the village is cut off?"

Ross considered that. "I don't know," he said finally, shaking his head, "I just don't know. If he's conditioned the people in the area to stay under his command by posthypnotics, then he could have turned it off. Or it may be that he's just using it nonstop until his techs crack what makes it tick."

"Wouldn't that be dangerous to them, or to the Chilean himself?" Walters queried.

This time it was Goldman who answered. "Think about it. When your boys developed it, they must have developed a countermeasure to enable them to use it. Part of the deal Chavez-Smith made to get hold of the chip must have included that."

"Is that what you were told?" Bolan pressed.

"Not as such," Goldman admitted, "but there was a definite implication."

"Can we afford to go with something that slim?" Grimaldi asked Bolan.

The soldier was grim-faced, his thoughts unreadable. Finally, he said, "We'll monitor the situation for a couple more hours. In the meantime, we prepare to move. Walters, you pin this down while the four of us get equipped."

NIGHT PASSED with the mercs being equipped and run through a few basic procedures by Bolan and Grimaldi. The combat bag was taken from its locker and placed in the back of the Citroën after Bolan used the contents to add additional inventory to the Smith & Wesson and Beretta that constituted the whole of the mercs' armory. Grimaldi was also equipped, and all four men donned blacksuits with working mikes. Bolan would have direct contact on a four-way basis with the other operatives, and they would also link up with Walters at base.

"We're going in by road, while Jack takes the chopper and waits just outside the dead zone—"

"The what?" Goldman interrupted.

"The dead zone," Bolan explained patiently. "The area surrounding the village of Santon. The dead area seems to extend in a circle for a couple kilometers in radius. Walters is pinpointing where it ends as accurately as possible. I want Jack outside with the chopper for immediate evac, and also for air backup if we have trouble. It's fully equipped with a cannon, right, Jack?"

"Yes," Grimaldi replied. "I'd have their hide if they'd given me anything else." There was something in the way the veteran flier said this that suggested he relished the chance to get away from the cinder-block bunker and out into the field.

"How are we going to deal with this if that dead zone is still in operation?"

"That's a difficult one. If this weapon works on frequency, then there must be headsets or earpieces that transmit a jamming frequency, so soldiers can use the weapon. The problem is that we don't know what that frequency is, so it's going to be impossible for us to protect ourselves until such time as we can capture a headset or earpiece from the enemy. In view of this, if the dead zone is still in effect, then we're going to have to keep watch on the border, and play the waiting game. If we have good recon, then we'll know if anyone's coming out, so the chances of Attaturk or Chavez-Smith escaping with the goods are reduced."

"I dunno if my nerves can take a long wait," Goldman mused. "I just want to get this sorted."

"We all want to get it sorted," Bolan snapped. "But if we have to wait, then we have to wait."

Leaving no room for any further argument, Bolan ended the briefing. The four men, now armed and ready for the upcoming battle, returned to base where Walters was waiting for them. The sun was beginning to rise as they walked across the dew-laden grass of the landing field. They had been there twenty-four hours—at least twenty longer than any of them could have hoped. In that time, Chavez-Smith could have offloaded the weapon to Attaturk—the presumed buyer, although there may well be other bidders—several times over. But the Chilean's greed, and his desire to take the chip apart and copy it, had bought them some time. Bolan, for his part, felt fresh and ready for the battle ahead.

He hoped the same could be said of Ross and Goldman.

Like it or not, he was relying on them to keep their end of the unspoken agreement, and act like soldiers.

When they entered the bunker and saw the look on Walters's face, Bolan knew it was all systems go.

"First details coming through from the village at 05:32. The gendarmerie contacted their regional command center. They were confused and after some kind of assistance. A small group from the local police has been detached to investigate. Apparently they know that they have been out of touch since yesterday around midday, but they can't remember a thing about what has happened in that time."

"Is it just the local police?"

Walters shook his head. "It's moving up. Everyone is coming around and realizing that people have been trying to get in touch."

"What's the situation like with the local police and the French army? Are there any emergency procedures to cover civil events like this?"

Walters nodded. "Yes, but none of the plans have ever been put into operation. There seems to be a lot of confusion at local level, and a distinct reluctance to go national, as it would expose some inadequacies. I'd say you've got a six-hour window before it blows up, Colonel."

"Thank God for bureaucracy."

14

Despite the increasing communication with the village of Santon, and the growing awareness of the strange events that had occurred over the previous twenty-four hours, there were no roadblocks yet established, and no increase in traffic toward the village. The roads remained virtually deserted, and Walters kept all four of the war party up to speed with events as he monitored them from the airfield.

"Chavez-Smith is no fool, and however arrogant he's become, he's going to realize that he has a limited time frame before his base is tracked down as the source of these events," Bolan said as he negotiated the narrow roads and hairpin turns that characterized the mostly rural area. The sun had risen on a landscape that could make a man realize why it had become a retreat. Given time to stop and consider, it would be bizarre that a place so beautiful could mask such evil intent.

But there was no time.

"If his buyer is Attaturk, then they will have done the majority of their business a couple of nights ago on the yacht, and maybe he's even there now to observe the tests, which could give us a problem," Bolan continued, before explaining all that the Countess D'Orsini had told him.

"You sly old dog, so that's what you were up to when it

went quiet," Grimaldi said over the com link. The pilot had been wondering for some time about that sudden silence during operations, and had made the obvious deduction.

"All in the line of business," Bolan replied with a grin. "Thing is, the last scenario we want is to be running into another assault team that's basically on the same side. They won't be after the same thing, but they want to put Attaturk and Chavez-Smith out of business."

"We've been monitoring Attaturk's movements," came Walters's voice from base. "He's still in Marseilles."

"That's good news," Bolan stated. "That means we're on our own against Hector."

"I hope so," Ross said from the back seat. "This is going to be enough of a fight as it is without another team interfering."

"Not getting scared are you, Errol?" Goldman asked.

"Damn right I am," Ross growled. "I'd be a fool if I wasn't."

"Right," Bolan affirmed. "The odds are heavily stacked against us. But I figure we can do it if we get the area secured then hit them hard."

"I'm looking forward to it," Goldman said softly.

That was what worried Bolan. The last thing he wanted was Goldman charging in like a rogue elephant when strategy was the key. The redhead was now heavily armed, and was aware of the amount of hardware carried in the combat bag that sat in the back of the car.

Why, the soldier asked himself, did he get the idea that Goldman could prove to be more of a problem that Chavez-Smith and Destiny's Spear combined?

But there was no time to think about it now. The car cornered another hairpin, dipping into a hollow that saw them surrounded by grassed banks covered in wildflowers, before emerging onto a straightaway that faced a small village. The road ran through the main street, which they could see clearly, revealing a few shops and stone houses, with a church and hotel, and some streets that led off this main thoroughfare. It was quiet, and there were very few people visible on the streets, despite the fact that life was usually in full swing early in such rural areas.

As they approached a signpost, Bolan stepped on the brake so that the sign would be more than just a passing blur.

They were entering Santon.

LEADING OFF THE NARROW main street was a small, enclosed village square, with a statue in the middle of some local dignitary, a bar that was closed, the town hall and the local gendarmerie. The street and sidewalk were deserted. Bolan pulled the car to halt and spoke into his mike.

"We've arrived in Santon. It's quiet here like they've been hit by the plague. Hopefully, the local police will still be too confused to ask too many questions, but before we hit the Chilean, I want to find out a little more about the effects of this weapon."

"Copy that," came Grimaldi's voice. "I'll be listening in. I've settled on the outskirts of the dead zone, about ten minutes' flying time from target location. I'll keep things ticking over here and wait for the word."

"Copy," Bolan replied. "What about you, Walters?"

"If you had time, I'd put some of what I'm getting on the line. These guys are in complete confusion, all trying to pass the buck to get in and investigate. I'd also figure that Chavez-Smith has some heavy money going into the pockets of some bureaucrats, as there's a distinct reticence to rubber-stamp an army operation."

"Wouldn't surprise me at all," Bolan answered. "But I guess we can't knock it if it buys us some time. If we get this right, then those corrupt officials will be going on cheaper vacations next year."

The Executioner got out of the car and headed toward the gendarmerie, with Ross and Goldman hot on his heels.

The small station was covered with posters concerned more with agricultural and social notices than police business. The worn wooden counter hadn't been replaced, and it was only the presence of a battered computer terminal and a modern phone that dragged the room, kicking and screaming, into the twenty-first century.

The front desk was empty as the three men entered. Bolan looked around, but there was no sign of activity. An old bell stood on the battered counter, and he banged it hard. The sound seemed unnaturally loud in the room. Nothing happened for a few seconds, and then they heard the sounds of movement from a room beyond. A gendarme emerged.

"Yes?" he asked, a little blankly. Then, as he took in the blacksuits and the hardware adorning the three men in front of him, his hand snaked to the holster at his hip.

"No," Bolan said, holding up both hands. "You're expecting us. You've been trying to get someone here for hours, right?"

Looking at the young man's blank expression, eyes staring and pupils dilated, even in the bright light of the room, Bolan had been immediately able to define that the young gendarme was still in a state of shock. His delayed reactions, and the slowness with which he had reacted to their presence, only served to reinforce that. Bolan had no wish to engage the man in pointless combat. He wasn't their enemy, but he was dazed enough to be fooled into thinking they were from a government agency, perhaps dazed enough to not ask for identification.

The gendarme's hand stopped on the way to the holster. He blinked once, then said in a voice that sounded as though he had awakened from a long sleep, "It's about time. Why don't you people want to help us?"

"We do. It's just taken us a little time to get here. Bureaucracy, you know?" Bolan said as he shrugged.

The young gendarme gave him a lopsided smile. "Oh yeah," he replied slowly, "I know all about that, if only from this morning. But then, I don't blame them. It all sounds so weird, even to me."

There was a wondering tone about the last sentence that alerted Bolan's combat sense. There was an added complication on the way, he was sure.

"Why, exactly, does it sound so strange?" he asked carefully.

The young gendarme seemed to take forever to frame an answer. He looked at the three men in turn and then down at himself. Finally, he looked up again, straight at Bolan.

"It's like this. I woke up this morning and I found that I am a gendarme, and I have been for some time according to the papers I found. Yet all I can remember is yesterday. And yesterday I was a farmhand, working out the summer in the hope of getting a place to train for this job. I can't remember a single thing that has taken place in the past year."

Bolan tried to control his amazement, but could tell that, behind him, Ross and Goldman had exchanged sharp glances.

"Are you the only one who feels this?" he asked, focusing intently on the gendarme. The young man was trying to cooperate, but it was obvious that he was still feeling the aftereffects of whatever had occurred in the village. He was struggling to think faster, react with more speed and intelligence. Seeing this, Bolan added, "Don't try too hard. We think we know what is responsible for what has happened. It uses sound and has a powerful posthypnotic effect. It may take you some time to return to normal. Your mind has had a terrible shock. Don't try to force it, just take your time."

Time was the one thing they didn't have, but to try to make the young gendarme respond too quickly could actually cause more delay in the long term. The young man gave a slow, relieved smile at the soldier's words.

"It may sound ridiculous to you, but I'm actually pleased you've told me that. It maybe goes toward explaining things. I shall try to tell you, as concisely as I can, what has happened since awakening this morning.

"It was still the early hours. Dawn had not quite broken. I was confused and could not get any orientation for a while. I remember wondering why I was here, and why the uniform. It made no sense to me. I am not the only man to work here— my colleague Jean-Paul is out checking the outlying farms to see what has happened there. Maybe I can raise him—"

"In a moment," Bolan interjected. "First, your story."

The young gendarme nodded. "Very good. I awoke very confused, and the first thing I did was to check if anyone else was in the building. It was empty. There is little crime out here, and I discovered from the roster pinned to the wall that Jean-Paul was at home. It was my turn to sit through the night shift. I also discovered that I have been here some months, and that it is not the year that I thought it to be. When Jean-Paul came in, he was surprised to see me naturally, and almost drew his pistol on me before I had a chance to explain.

"Neither of us knew what had happened, but one thing was for sure—it was odd, and that it would worry and confuse the people when they were roused. And if we were awake, then they soon would be. It was then that we decided that Jean-Paul must make the rounds of all the outlying farms, and before that check around Santon. I would stay here and try to raise the authorities and get some action. People would not be expecting to see me—to them I was still a farmhand barely out of being a teenager. They would expect Jean-Paul or Jacques."

"Jacques is another gendarme, I take it. Where is he right now?" Bolan asked.

The young gendarme paused, pursed his lips as though composing himself. "That is the tragedy. Jacques was well-liked around here, and there must have been much grieving at the time. You see, the reason that I am now a gendarme here is because Jacques was killed ten months ago in a car accident."

Bolan knew the grief following death, and felt a pang for those who would have to grieve all over again—particularly the man's family, if they were still resident.

"I know this must be incredibly difficult for you to take in right now," the soldier began, "but coming from the outside we know the total area affected. I'll give you the map references, and you can contact your colleague so he knows the radius. I also need to talk to him to check if everyone he has come across so far has suffered in the same way. Can you do that for me?"

"Sure," the young gendarme agreed. "He should be out at the Château Soleil about now. That's been rented out by an Englishman—"

Bolan stopped the young gendarme with a raised. "What? Get him, now. Find out if he's there, and don't say a word about us until you know."

"What—" began the confused young man.

"We think the problem may originate from there, and it's vital that the inhabitants know nothing about our presence in the area."

"But if you know what is going on, then why are there only three of you, and—"

Bolan cut him short. "We're an advance party, scouting the ground. There'll be others after us." And he was not lying to the gendarme. However, the others wouldn't be pleased if they ran into the soldier and his two companions, and with luck Bolan would have called in Grimaldi and completed evac before the French army rolled into town.

The gendarme took them at face value, nodding shortly and beckoning them into the back room of the small gendarmerie, where a shortwave set stood waiting. The three men waited restlessly while he attempted to raise his colleague. The first two attempts yielded no result, and the men exchanged glances loaded with meaning. If this Jean-Paul had stumbled into the lair of the Chilean, then the terrorists acting as a private army would be on red alert, and Bolan's task would be that much more difficult.

The third time, the set crackled into life, and Jean-Paul answered. The young gendarme's name was Phillipe, and he exchanged a brief and garbled explanation with his older colleague when it was revealed that the Château Soleil was the next port of call on Jean-Paul's list. It took some convincing from the younger man before Jean-Paul was forced to drop his wild idea of scouting the ground for the advance team.

Eventually, Jean-Paul settled for speaking to Bolan, filling him in on what he had discovered on his rounds. It would appear that the effects of the weapon had been uniform, so it didn't diminish in strength over distance. This meant that the cutoff point hadn't been arbitrary, it had been carefully planned. The weapon was far more accurate and powerful than the soldier had imagined—and far more dangerous. They would have to move immediately.

Bolan gave the gendarme map references for the points where the dead zone had been known to have ended. This would help Jean-Paul plan his route more efficiently, and it would also keep him away from the three-man team as they mounted their assault.

The older gendarme signed off, and Phillipe turned to the men.

"Is there anything I can do to help?" he asked. "I resent these bastards taking a year from my life."

Bolan shook his head. "This has been a major piece of psychological warfare. You've been subjected to an immense strain, and you must realize yourself that your reflexes aren't running at a hundred percent." The gendarme nodded, and Bolan continued, "This operation will demand complete concentration and fast reflexes. The people we suspect to be behind this are a highly skilled terrorist operation. It's imperative that we hit them hard and fast. You would be a danger to yourself as much as to us right now, but don't think that I don't appreciate your courage and determination. A good soldier knows when to step back."

The gendarme nodded. "Yes, I do still feel…I don't know, like I'm not myself, yet. Yeah, you're right. Is there *anything* I can do?"

"You can sit here and wait. You're an important liaison with your colleague. Whatever else happens, the two of you must keep the local population from going near the château. None of us want innocent people injured or killed. You've got to hold the fort while we scout the area and wait for the main body of troops to arrive. And believe me, that's vitally important right now."

The gendarme nodded as Bolan turned to leave.

Bolan led Ross and Goldman out to the car.

"Jesus, you fed him a line there," Goldman said.

Bolan fixed him with a stare. "Not really. There will be other forces. And I don't want innocent parties getting in the way. I want this finished quickly and as cleanly as possible. Is that understood?"

He held Goldman's stare until the merc looked away.

15

The Château Soleil stood seven kilometres outside of Santon, and it took Bolan less than a quarter of an hour to find
the walls that surrounded the southern side of the estate. A
minor vineyard producing red wine for export, it consisted
of several acres of grapevines set within a protective environment, with two main outbuildings and the sprawling
château itself set almost dead center within the grounds.

They had a layout of the property that Grimaldi had pulled
off estate management files via e-mail attachments—Grimaldi
also carried a copy of this with him in his chopper—and knew
that Chavez-Smith had picked his inland base well. It had a
lot of cover and several good surveillance points. It would take
any force some time to penetrate the natural defenses.

Bolan drove past the wall to the south, taking the next two
right turns, down a narrow road and then a dirt track leading
to a closed gate, before bringing the car to a halt.

"Jack, do you copy?" Bolan said into the blacksuit mike.

"Yeah, I copy," Grimaldi replied.

Bolan reported their position, so Grimaldi could locate
them on the map. The soldier now had his copy spread across
his lap. He continued, "The walls themselves seem to be
fairly old—red brick covering repairs on old stone, filled in

with small rocks and pebbles in concrete. They look much as you'd expect the walls on one of these old places to look. Interesting thing is that there was no sign on this wall of any recent repairs. It all seemed to be well-weathered. If the Chilean was going to put any cameras or infrared onto the walls, no matter how well-disguised it was, the work would still seem new. After all, he hasn't been there long."

"Copy that," Grimaldi said. "What about road embankments?"

"Fairly steep. The distance from road to wall is less than a foot, and the undergrowth is sparse, mostly grasses and wildflowers."

"What is this, a botany lesson?" Goldman growled.

"Leave it, Jimmy, this is serious business," Ross snapped.

Bolan ignored them and continued. "Hiding anything in that small a space, with that little cover to play around with, would take a lot of time and planning. He hasn't had that, though I have no doubt he's got the equipment."

"Which means you figure that it's all there once you get over the wall, right?"

"Yes. From what we already know, there's wild land and then ordered rows of vineyard before we reach the outbuildings or the main building. That's plenty of cover for a lot of security, whether it's electronic or human. Getting over the wall is no problem, but once over…"

"What's the plan?" Grimaldi asked.

"I plan to go over first, do a recon. If I can work out what level of defense he has on this sector, then it's a reasonable working assumption that the same will apply on all four quarters."

"What do you need from me?" the pilot asked.

"Just the usual, Jack, for now. If it gets too hot and I say the word, come get me."

"Roger."

Bolan then turned to Ross and Goldman. "Do we have any problem with that?" However, he already knew the answer from the expression on the redhead's face. Goldman was grim and serious, trying hard to contain his explosive anger.

"Yeah, I do have just a tiny problem," he said tightly. "If you go over on your own, what's to stop you getting the chip and then have laughing boy pick you up while we sit here like idiots?"

"Nothing," Bolan replied, "except that it'll take a hell of a lot of luck and bucking the odds for me to get to the château entirely by myself without being taken out by who knows what security. It'd be tantamount to a suicide mission, and only something I'd do in an emergency situation. And this, my friend, is not one of those."

"I think one of us should go with you on this so-called reconnaissance, keep an eye on you," Goldman grumbled.

Bolan held his temper. The mercenary's distrust was annoying, especially in view of the fact that Bolan could have taken out either of them on numerous occasions, and there was, in fact, no necessity for either Ross or Goldman to have been allowed to leave the airfield. Walters had the manpower—discreetly placed, but noticeable to the trained eye such as the Executioner's—to restrain or eliminate them both.

The soldier spoke slowly, allowing his words to sink in. "The purpose of a recon is to scout the land and take as little risk as possible. Since neither of you has the training or experience that I can trust, it would be asking for trouble to take either of you with me. It would be like making an assault without planning. If you want to do that, then I call up Jack, we get a force from the USAF base using the security clearances we have, and we cause an international incident. You wouldn't want that, would you?"

"Of course not, then we wouldn't get our hands on the chip," Goldman blustered.

"Same result, whether we do it that way or your way. Is that perfectly clear, now?" Bolan asked.

Ross had been watching both Bolan and his partner carefully during the exchange. Now he chose to speak. "Jimmy, let the man do it his way. He hasn't lied to us once so far, and what he says makes sense. Remember, man, you might not trust him, but he doesn't have to trust us, either—and he has, so far."

Goldman, still fuming, looked long and hard at his partner, as though silently cursing him for selling him out. Finally, he said through visibly gritted teeth, "Fine, have it your way. But don't blame me if it fucks up on us."

"It won't. I need you as much as you need me. That's the only reason this is working," Bolan said. "Give me twenty minutes max, then you can come after me if you want."

"Sounds fair," Ross agreed.

Without another word, the soldier left them in the car, his mind already focused on his mission.

BOLAN VAULTED THE GATE and cut across the field to the hedgerow facing the road. It provided him with ample cover from which to examine the length of the old wall opposite. There were overhanging trees that blocked the top of the wall, the jutting branches making it a difficult, though not impossible, climb. That wasn't the problem. Did the trees harbor any traps, or any security devices that may alert the enemy to his presence? Bolan wondered

Scanning the length of the wall, he could see no visible signs. The trees were overhanging so densely that to position cameras or infrared so that they could make an effective line of sight would be virtually impossible. Not without some major tree surgery, and even it was skillfully managed, it would still be visible among the wildness of the old growth.

Any electronic defenses would be operational once he was over the wall. Picking his spot, Bolan slipped out of the cover of the hedges at a point where the brush was at its thinnest, and quickly crossed the road. He sprinted up the steep bank and flattened himself to the wall, edging along it to a point where two overhanging oaks had fought for space, the branches having the thinnest of growth and the most air between them of anywhere along the wall. In truth, it was such a good natural defense that there was no need for the Chilean to bother with extra measures. Even at this narrow point, Bolan would still have to fight his way through.

He turned and searched for foot- and handholds. He was acutely aware that on this side of the wall he was plainly visible to any who passed by—and even if they were not attached to Chavez-Smith or Destiny's Spear, they may feel it their duty to report an intruder to the Englishman who was renting the château.

The wall, with its many repairs over the years, was a simple climb. The patchwork of stone, brick and concrete gave an ample amount of holds for him to reach the top of the twelve-foot wall in no time. Tentatively, he felt along the top of the wall for wires, broken glass, or any other kind of obstruction. There was nothing except the overhanging branches, and even at this point, where they were at their sparsest, they still pushed out and blocked the top of the wall, making it impossible for the soldier to climb straight over.

Aware that time was of the essence, and that he was vulnerable to attack or view from the road below, Bolan clung to the wall with one hand while using the other to search for some kind of handhold in the foliage. The leaves were fresh, the sap oozing from the branches as the bark stripped in his hand. It was too slippery, too young and weak to hold his weight.

He would have to take risks. He dropped his free hand from the branches toward the blacksuit and unsheathed the Tekna knife. He hacked at some of the younger shoots, clearing a small space on top of the wall. He sheathed the knife and took a firm grip of the wall, hauling himself into the small space and using his powerful shoulders to push against the stronger branches that lay beneath. It took an immense effort, and he couldn't relax for a second or else the branches would spring back and push him away from the wall. Finally he was able to bring his other hand up and secure himself against the top of the wall. The branches gathered around, pushing back down on him.

The soldier pulled the rest of his body onto the wall, forcing back the covering branches as he straddled the top of the barrier. It was difficult to see past the thick covering of branches to the ground below, but it looked to be a farther drop than the climb. The steep bank on the road side of the wall had been built up, perhaps to shore up the wall's foundations. Bolan judged the other side to be about seventeen to eighteen feet. An awkward enough distance for him to sprain an ankle, or break a leg if he fell badly. And this was possible when the ground below was hidden by the foliage. Through the dense screen, all he could see was a layer of bracken and grasses that could have been an inch or a foot deep.

Sliding over, Bolan lowered himself until he was at full stretch, hanging by his fingertips from the top of the wall. It was still a long drop. He took a deep breath and let go. He was braced for the shock of impact and let himself crumple, knees bending to absorb that shock, ready to roll with the momentum of his fall.

The ground beneath was springy, the grasses and ferns providing a cushion that lessened the impact. He rolled and came up on his feet. Stretching muscles, he was relieved to find that nothing had been damaged.

Bolan turned his attention to the surrounding grounds. The scrub and wilderness petered out toward large walls of vine, heavy with grapes as the season reached its apex. Somehow, he doubted if there was any intention to produce wine this year. But the flowering and fruiting vines provided good cover for the château and its outbuildings, which were barely visible in the distance. It was a lot of ground to scout, and although it provided the Executioner with good cover, it also provided ample protection for any security patrol.

Bolan made his way across the scrub. He unleathered the Beretta and fitted a sound suppressor as he advanced, so that the 9 mm Parabellum rounds would sound as little more than a cough if he was forced to use it. But even that would be noticeable in the silence of the morning, and he hoped that he would be able to evade any patrols. A missing man or the sound of a firefight was the last thing he wanted. His aim was to slip in and out without being noticed.

As he advanced, alert for movement around him, he kept his eyes open at ground level for any infrared or camera equipment. This made his progress slower than he would have wished, but it was an imperative if he wanted to evade detection. Yet, despite his vigilance, he saw no evidence that the grounds had been seeded with security devices.

Perhaps the Chilean had intended this merely as land base rather than a secure war base, and had only been forced into this by the concurrent arrival of both Bolan and the mercs in Marseilles? It was a thought, and would account for his pulling back the remainder of the Destiny's Spear cell to the château. They were to be the only security, with strength in numbers.

Bolan by no means gave up on scanning the ground for cameras and infrared, but he relaxed a little, and concentrated the majority of his attention on spotting security patrols.

He was soon rewarded.

By this time he had made his way around to the far eastern side and was closing in on the walls of vines. He came out of the scrub and began to move among the fruit and leaves, rustling in the gentle breeze that scented the air with a sweet tang. It was so peaceful and beautiful that it was hard to believe that a group of terrorists headed by an international arms dealer was on site.

But just when it seemed to be too good, reality struck a blow. As he rounded the end of one long wall of vine, the soundproofing it offered suddenly cut out, and Bolan could hear approaching footsteps. He moved back, crouching and slipping the safety off the Beretta.

Bolan almost held his breath, breathing shallowly as he heard the footsteps approach. There was a low mumble of conversation.

"That was really stupid, telling her you'd bring her here. What if someone heard you?"

"Paul, you worry far too much. I didn't tell her exactly where we were. I was only keeping the whining bitch quiet."

"It doesn't matter, Emil. If Hector gets wind of this, then you're dead, you know that?"

"Well, I won't tell him if you won't."

"Yeah, right. Anyway, we're not supposed to be talking like we're having a quiet stroll. What if we're heard?"

"By whom? You really think there's anyone around?"

The two men walked past the end of the vine and turned toward the house. Little did Emil Herve know that he had been overheard *twice*, Bolan thought. It was fortunate he had been such a weak link in the chain of Destiny's Spear.

The soldier counted ten, then followed in their direction. If he was to their rear, there was little chance of such slack sentries looking back and discovering him. Meanwhile, they would give him a clear passage on the rest of his recon.

He followed them to the front of the château, only hanging back when the cover became more sparse. He would have to double back to get a look at the west wall, as the north was far too open for attack, consisting mostly of a manicured lawn and a carefully sculptured garden with a long drive leading to the main gates. It did, however, give him his first clear view of the château and the outbuildings. They looked open to attack, with nothing to protect them except the terrorists themselves. The outbuildings were little more than barns, open to the elements at the windows and doors, with only wooden shutters to protect them. And the château itself was a maze of windows and doors opening onto the drive and gardens, a nightmare to defend, which was why so many of the Destiny's Spear gunners were standing guard, cradling rifles and SMGs but paying scant attention to the area beyond the front of the building.

However, there was one thing about them that made Bolan change his mind about scouting the west wall. All of them, including the two he had followed, were wearing headsets. These were not standard security communications headsets with radio mikes attached. They were clumsier, although still

small, and looked like the frequency blockers Ross and Goldman had described.

The fact that everyone in sight was wearing them suggested that another test was imminent. Bolan had to get out.
If he and the mercs were to strike, they had to move quickly
over the wall, and also try to take out some guards and get
their headsets.

More pressing than that, if the test began in the next few
minutes, Bolan could be caught cold on enemy territory, paralyzed and trapped with the enemy still moving freely....

16

Bolan made his way back through the maze of vines and into the wilderness as swiftly as he could. He had to weigh the possibility of being caught in the test against being caught by guards if he was too reckless. The guards being the more immediate danger, he avoided the temptation to make a straight run, and followed the route he had taken, where he knew the areas of cover. There was, however, little for him to worry about. The Destiny's Spear terrorists were slack as a private army, and their lack of discipline and training meant that they were too busy relaxing by the château to bother with anything other than a cursory patrol.

As he made his way back to the south wall, Bolan pondered this. Certainly, Signella would have knocked them into shape if he was alive. As it stood, Chavez-Smith was probably too immersed in his tests, and the need to complete them before handing over the chip, to notice that his so-called defense wasn't as encompassing as he had hoped. The negative side of this, for the soldier, was twofold. First, it concentrated forces around the area he had hoped to crack easily, and second it made obtaining a protective headset difficult. He had hoped that they would be able to cut a swath through the defenses and then take out the remainder piece by piece after attaining the objective. Now it would be a cluster of firefights, giving the Chilean a chance to get away or trigger the sonic weapon while Bolan and the mercs were bogged down. And if there were few guards on patrol, it made the chances of taking some out and then using their headsets that much greater.

Bolan moved freely through the undergrowth to the wall, knowing that there were no security and surveillance devices for him to trigger. All he had to worry about was the wall.

When he reached it, he paused, working out the quickest way to get up and over. From this side, it was eighteen feet at most, and scanning the area of wall surrounding and beneath the gap in the branches that he had made earlier, he could see that although there were copious amounts of hand- and footholds, the wall on this side had been attacked by moss and lichen. The road side of the wall was fairly dry, but this was much more slippery, and the dampness may have eaten into the mortar that bound the stone and brick together. He gave an experimental tug at one of the most likely holds and felt it give beneath his strength. With his full weight on it, it was likely to crumble completely. A few more experiments of that nature, and he determined that the wall wasn't safe on this side.

Bolan stepped back and looked at the oaks whose sturdy, overhanging branches would support his weight and allow him to get onto the top of the wall.

He allowed himself a small smile. Buildings, walls, mountains, but it had been a long time since he'd been tree climbing.

Testing a lower limb for weight-bearing, he hauled himself up onto the body of the tree, moving swiftly upward until he reached those branches and limbs that were drifting across toward the wall. None of them seemed strong enough to hold him, but there was one that was thick and strong as it joined the trunk, and he stood upright, edging out a few inches until the wall was within jumping distance.

Bolan leaped for the wall, rolling across it as he landed heavily, feeling the uneven stone and brick along the top bite into him. His momentum carried him over the top of the wall, and he held on as he toppled over, fingers and palms biting into the brick and stone to keep him from a freefall. His torso thudded against the wall, and he waited until the shock wave had passed before allowing himself to drop slowly, making sure he kept his footing on the steep bank.

All the while he had kept silent, even though the mike on the blacksuit would have enabled him to give Grimaldi and the mercs a running commentary. From what he'd seen, he didn't want to panic Goldman into a rash action, which, he felt, would be too easy. But now he chose to speak, to allow them to know his movements.

"Ross, Goldman, be ready to move. I'm on the outside and heading your way. Jack, keep tuned in and get ready."

"Copy that," Grimaldi replied briefly.

Bolan crossed the road and went through the hedgerow, cutting across the fields to the Citroën. As he neared the car, he saw that both Ross and Goldman were out in the open, looking expectantly toward him.

"Well?" the redhead asked impatiently as Bolan approached.

"First thing is that we need to move now. I suspect Chavez-Smith has another test of some kind planned. All the guards I saw had on headsets. What we have to do is get some of those. If we can, then we have a chance."

"We'd have a better chance if you sent your friend in to knock the crap out of them with some of the hardware I'm betting he's got on that chopper of his," Goldman said heatedly.

"Don't be an idiot," Bolan answered harshly. "They'd see the chopper coming in and use the weapon. With Jack immobilized, the chopper goes down, and they know there are other forces imminent—other forces that would also be immobilized. The only way to do this is with stealth. And we'll just have to hope that we can get in there and get headsets before the test."

"If we don't?" Ross queried.

"It's a chance we'll have to take," Bolan said simply. "One advantage we will have is that there's no way they'll be expecting an attack during a test, so we get headsets and attack them during the test itself. And believe me, we'll need every advantage we can get…"

Briefly, Bolan outlined the situation beyond the walls of the estate. It soon became obvious that the solution would be to draw the terrorists from out of the château and outbuildings and into the vineyards, where their strength would be dissipated. But this couldn't be done until they had obtained headsets.

"How are we going to do that?" Goldman asked.

"Hang on, wait," Ross countered, "if Cooper followed one security patrol, then they must be circulating at regular intervals, right?"

"I'd say so," Bolan replied. "I did a quick head count, and from that I figure there's always eight to ten men on the grounds, most likely in pairs like the patrol I followed. That way, there's always a sector of the grounds that's covered."

"So how does that help us? There's three of us and only two in a patrol. That doesn't add up," Goldman said.

Bolan shook his head. "We don't go in together. We split and take the east, west and south. The northern approach is completely open, and would be a suicide mission. The way I figure it is that we go over the wall at the point where we already have an opening, then split up and take a sector each.

We can keep in touch with the mikes," he added, tapping the mike in his blacksuit, "and search out the patrols in each sector. Hit them hard, get a headset, and when they're in place we synchronize and mount the attack."

"Sounds like a straightforward plan," Ross said, "but how are you going to draw them out of the château and disperse their forces?"

"Well, if we synchronize and hit them from three angles, they'll be like headless chickens anyway," Bolan answered, "but just to stir them up a little more, I've got this."

The soldier moved to the trunk of the car, opened it and lifted out the combat bag. He set it on the ground and withdrew a disassembled weapon. Goldman looked at Ross, puzzled. Ross shrugged. Neither recognized it.

"Gentlemen, say hello to the M-16 A-2, complete with an M-203 grenade launcher riding beneath. When this is put together, it takes a full thirty rounds of 5.56 mm ammunition. I guarantee this'll will get the hornets out of the nest."

"Damn, it would make me move quickly." Ross whistled softly. "How long does it take to assemble?"

"Not long," Bolan answered. "The only thing is getting the combat bag over the wall, with the trees providing such a strong natural defense. That's one of the reasons I want us to go over in the same place. It'll make stowing this a lot quicker if we work it between us."

"Sounds good to me," Ross said. "Let's do it."

The three men exchanged glances. With combat about to begin, any differences were put aside for the common goal. They knew that there would be dispute over the chip if and when they obtained it, but that could wait. If they were to stand any chance of getting through this alive, then they would have to pull together.

Without a word, Bolan led them across the fields and out onto the road. There was no sign of any passing traffic—idly, Bolan wondered if this road ever saw more than one car or truck in a day—and they crossed over to the wall.

"I'll go first," Bolan said briefly. "When I'm on top, pass up the combat bag."

He found the foot- and handholds that had served him so well on his first climb, and hoisted himself onto the wall. It was easier now, with the space made by the hacked away young shoots, and the knowledge of how the limbs pushed at him. He straddled the wall and attempted to sit upright, his spine forcing some of the heavy foliage back and clear of the wall, making a space for the combat bag.

"Okay," he said. Goldman and Ross both lifted the heavy bag until it came within the soldier's grasp. He took hold of it, feeling the strain in his biceps and forearm muscles as the deadweight of the hardware tried to drag his arm downward, out of its socket. He gritted his teeth and slowly began to lift.

With a slow but steady movement, the bag attained the crest of the wall, and Bolan paused only for a fraction of a second, before using his other hand to grasp the handles of the bag and let it fall over the other side. It landed with a dull thump in the bracken and grasses, which he knew would cushion the impact of its fall.

"Okay, follow me," he said to Ross and Goldman before allowing himself to drop onto the other side, landing in a roll beside the combat bag. He rose to his feet and moved to one side, taking the bag with him. The last thing he wanted was either of the mercs to land on the heavy hardware and injure himself before the mission had even begun.

On the road side of the wall, Ross had started to climb. He pushed against the outgrowth of oak as he reached the top and marveled at the strength Bolan had to have to enable him to move against the limbs so easily. He heaved himself over the wall, dropping and rolling, stifling a grunt as he hit the ground. Even as he moved over to the château side of the wall, Goldman was following him up. The smaller redhead found it easier to squeeze into the gap Bolan had created, and he jumped away from the wall, rolling and coming upright with no problem.

Bolan led the way to the edge of the trees, beckoning them to follow. Quietly, knowing that raised voices would carry across the scrub and vineyard, he outlined the territory ahead and to the east. He ordered Goldman to take the east, and Ross to press on ahead, outlining the obstacles they may encounter, and reiterating the points of cover.

"What about you?" Ross asked.

"I'll take the west. It's the only area I haven't checked, and I can't send either of you into the unknown."

"But what if the château is protected to the west?" Ross continued. "What if you can't use that?" And he indicated the combat bag with the dismantled M-16/M-203 combo.

Bolan shook his head. "I could see enough to tell that the château is uncovered on all sides. There are enough windows in that building to make it a sun trap—and that's exactly what the original owners wanted. The outbuildings are far enough away to insure that, but not far enough for me not to be able to resight on them rapidly," he added with a sly grin. "Besides, when I use this, it'll bring them out into the open."

"Okay, let's get going, then."

"Only break radio silence to confirm you've obtained a headset, or in the event of emergency. Then we synchronize and attack. Understood?"

The mercs nodded and began to move out as Bolan turned

away, beginning to jog through the undergrowth in an arc around to the western side of the estate.

IN MANY WAYS, Errol Ross had the simplest task, as he had to move forward in a straight line for the shortest distance, but, unlike the others, this would entail moving across a far more open stretch of ground.

There were clumps of cover, but the area between the scrub and the maze of vines from the south was completely open for about a hundred yards. If Ross was caught by a guard patrol crossing this distance, there would be nowhere to hide.

Ross advanced as far as the edge of the scrub with ease and then hunkered down in cover. As he fitted a sound suppressor to his Beretta, he gave the surrounding area a careful surveillance. It looked deserted.

Rising into a crouch, Ross began to move swiftly across the empty area, his heart pounding in his ears and adrenaline racing through his veins. He wanted to catch a patrol so he could get a headset, but only when he was able to use some cover.

The entrance into the vineyard maze loomed before him, the convergence of three separated strands of vine coming together and then leaving a gap before the next set of twisting leaf and branch began. Of course, the other thing he didn't want to do was dive for the covering vines and run slap bang into a patrol when he wasn't prepared to fight. He slowed, trying to see as wide an angle as possible. It looked deserted, but...

No time for doubts. Ross took the corner made by the vines and proscribed an arc with the Beretta, his finger resting on the trigger, ready to tap a burst at the first sign of life.

Nothing.

Breathing a sigh of relief, he sank onto his haunches and

drew air into his lungs, willing his pounding heart to slow. But still he kept a sharp lookout for any security patrols. From what Cooper had told him, they were casual, obviously not expecting anyone. Ross still wanted to be first on the draw, the one who was the sharpest.

Getting to his feet, he set off toward the château, following the line of the vineyard maze, keeping his attention focused on any extraneous sounds.

He didn't have to wait long.

Ross had moved about two hundred yards into the maze when the sound of a laugh jolted him. It was about five hundred yards away, and as the laugh was followed by voices, he could hear that it was moving toward him. To the right or left? He strained to locate it exactly. To the right, nearer the château. There were two voices, and their French was too guttural and colloquial for him to make out what they were saying.

It didn't matter. The important thing was that they were headed his way. He had to take them out without their becoming aware of his presence.

Looking at his options, he could see that if he moved toward them, there was a very good chance that they would hear him, no matter how careful he was. Casting a glance over his shoulder, he could see that there was a break in the vine just behind him. That may just give him the edge.

The leaves and grapes were of such a thickness on the vines that Ross couldn't see through the wall of greenery. Logically, the same would apply to the guards passing on the other side. Even so, he still held his breath and crouched as he heard them draw level. They were still talking, and he could pick out a few words. They were being uncomplimentary about Chavez-Smith, and questioning the species of his parentage before moving on to complain about how long they would be stuck at the château. This topic of conversation kept them talking until they had passed beyond Ross.

With infinite care, he turned on his heel and brought up the Beretta so that it was leveled at them. He had hoped that the angle of the gap would be such that he would be able to tap the trigger and take them out without giving them a chance to turn. No such luck. By the time he was in position, one of them was hidden from view by the vines.

He didn't even take the time to curse. With one elongated stride he was at the gap and moving through. He brushed against the leaves, making them rustle. It was enough to alert the two guards to an alien presence, and they began to turn.

Not quickly enough. Four holes appeared in the two bodies, stretched across their backs. The slugs had to have taken out their kidneys, and bone splinters and shock waves damaged the remainder of their internal organs, especially at a range of only a couple of yards. Both men spun, the momentum of their turns increased by the force of the 9 mm Parabellum rounds as they hit home.

Even in the quiet vineyard, the sound-suppressed Beretta was nowhere near as loud as Ross had feared. He breathed a sigh of relief that neither of the guards had been prepared to fire, and there were no death spasms to trigger off useless bursts of SMG fire from the Uzi and H&K MP-5 that they were carrying.

As they hit the ground, Ross was already on the move. He checked that both were truly dead before advancing enough to bend over one of the guards and take off his headset. He fitted it to his own ears, finding that the earpiece for the blacksuit mike was proving something of an obstruction. As he removed the MP-5 from the dead guard and slung it over his shoulder—it would be a useful addition—he spoke quietly and rapidly into the mike.

"Ross. Two guards down and I have a headset. Can't wear it properly without removing the mike earpiece. Maybe should wait until after synchronization."

"Copy. Good point," Bolan's voice came back.

Ross said nothing more. He had a position to obtain before they were ready to attack, and two dead bodies made the likelihood of discovery greater.

Errol Ross hid the corpses in the vines and moved quickly toward the château.

JIMMY GOLDMAN WASN'T happy. This whole mission had been a crock as far as he was concerned. This guy Cooper, for one—the guy that the USAF lieutenant called Colonel Stone—who was he? Goldman wondered. This was supposed to have been a simple retrieval in Marseilles, and then away. Instead, this guy had gotten in their way. They'd been involved in a bloodbath, dragged over half of southern France—or so it seemed—and now he found himself running around the grounds of a château playing soldiers against a bunch of terrorists who, as far as he could work out, outnumbered them about ten to one.

Just great. Meanwhile, Ross was treating Cooper like he was God's gift to the intelligence business, and happily joining in with all the madness.

Goldman moved around the estate to the eastern edges, using the wild area as cover. It was excellent cover, all right, but he was more at home in the city, and it bothered him that he may pitch over on this uneven ground—with grass so thick he couldn't see where he was treading, or where there may be holes—and break his ankle. A lot of good he'd be then.

Goldman was itching for a guard to come into view. He badly wanted to kill something or someone to vent his anger. He could feel it boiling up in him to the point where he was literally seeing a red mist clouding everything. He stopped and tried to compose himself. This feeling wouldn't get the chip back. And not only did he need to be on form for that, he also needed to be on top of the game for when they had to deal with Cooper. He'd sure want to take possession of the chip, and Ross and Goldman's employers weren't likely to be too keen on that idea.

Looking around, he could see that he'd covered a lot of territory. He had to be more or less at the central point on the eastern wall. Just as well that he'd stopped where he was, or else he may have ended up coming around to the north wall, and the area that had been described as open. Now he had to get into the vines, across a hundred yards of open territory. Of course, he thought bitterly, that was no problem for Colonel Marvel, who could probably do it backward, and with his eyes closed.

The one thing Goldman had always been good at was running. Right from the days when he was a schoolboy athlete. And despite his age, he was still incredibly fit. The scrub separating the wild undergrowth from the vines was flat, almost grassless in places. He could see every little bump and dip. Goldman grinned to himself. This part of the advance he felt confident about; the rest could wait.

Checking that the land was clear as far as he could see and hear, Goldman gathered himself, then set off across the hundred yards of open ground. He treated it as though it were a race, which in some ways it was. Having checked before beginning, he didn't bother to look around as he ran, focusing totally on achieving the distance in a fast time.

He grunted as he reached the vines and managed to stop himself before he cannoned into them. He suppressed the desire to noisily gulp in great lungfuls of air after his exertion, consciously slowing his intake and trying to calm his racing heart. He crouched and looked around, suddenly realizing that anyone could be approaching while he remained that oblivious.

Fortunately, the surrounding area was still empty.

Taking a moment to compose himself, he heard Ross's voice in his earpiece. Ross had a headset and was warning them about the blacksuit mikes. He also heard Cooper's brief reply. Should he say anything? No, wait until he had something to report. He'd have to move fast, though.

For Goldman, this summed up how he felt about the way this mission had turned out. How stupid was it that he'd spent this long avoiding a security patrol, and now he desperately needed one?

Only one way to do that, as far as he could see. Part of his armory was an MP-5, and he unslung it and checked the clip. Full. He made sure it was seated. The hardware was ready, he was hyped up.

Time to go hunting.

Goldman moved along the outside edge of the vine, traveling north and looking for a gap in the maze through which to enter. He found a hole, and he took it with the MP-5 raised and ready.

Both directions were clear. He stopped and listened.

Nothing. So which direction should he head in search of a patrol? Did they move clockwise or counterclockwise?

Mentally, he flipped a coin and got counterclockwise. Shrugging, he moved off quickly, keeping an ear open for approaching security.

He didn't have to wait too long. He'd only gone a couple of hundred yards before he heard them approach. Two voices, one male and one female. Heavy, ponderous footsteps. Goldman's French was even more limited than that of his partner, but he could tell by the dragging feet and the bored tones that these were two guards whose attention was anything but focused on their task.

Good. That should make his task easier.

They were about to round a bend in a path running between the vines, heading straight toward him. Goldman pulled himself into the nearside of the bend, so that their angle of vision wouldn't catch him until the last minute, and then raised the MP-5, ready to fire. There was no suppressor on the SMG, and he knew that in this silence the noise would carry back to the château with a cover-shattering ease, but right then he didn't care. He just wanted the headset before the next trial began.

The woman was in her early twenties, thickset with heavy breasts and splaying hips barely contained by her jeans. She wore wire-rimmed glasses and an angry expression that was frozen into surprise as she caught sight of Goldman waiting for her. The man by her side was slightly older, taller and much thinner. He had an arm around her shoulders as he talked. Both of them had their SMGs at a downward angle, and were completely unprepared for what was about to greet them. In fact, the man didn't even get a chance to look up before he died.

Goldman squeezed the trigger of the MP-5 and seven shots rang out so closely that they could have been one. They drilled the two guards from the top of the man's shoulder to the woman's hip, running in a ragged diagonal line. The heavy shells ripped flesh, bone and soft internal tissue as they drove through the two bodies. The momentum threw the two bodies backward, and before they had even hit the dirt, Goldman was on them. He took a headset from the girl and placed it on his head. He could hear the echo of his shots dying away on the air, and was damned sure that they could hear them in the château. Pausing to listen, he could hear nothing reach him by way of response or disturbance, but knew that it was only a matter of time.

"Goldman. I've got a headset and eliminated two guards," he said briefly.

"Yeah, I kind of gathered that," came Ross's sardonic tones. "Why not let them know we're here, Jimmy?"

Cooper's voice broke in. He was trying to hold his temper, but the anger was apparent in his voice, which only served to make Goldman grin.

"Dammit, Goldman, we were supposed to be in position before letting them know we were here. We'll have to move fast. Wait to hear from me. Out."

BOLAN'S OWN JOURNEY had been harder. Although the mercs hadn't been in the château grounds before, they had the intel from the soldier's recon to guide them. But the western side of the estate was the one that Bolan hadn't been able to scan before having to make for the outside. And so it was that much harder for him to make rapid progress, especially as he was carrying the combat bag containing the M-16/M-203 combo.

The territory over this sector was much the same as before. The wilderness that had been allowed to develop around the walls provided him with good cover as he moved around the perimeter, allowing him to remain hidden. He kept a close watch on the maze of vines but saw little activity. The security patrols were obviously there, but they saw no reason to cover the area beyond the maze of vines, perhaps figuring that the expanse of bare land between wilderness and vine would act as its own security.

Wrong.

The wilderness was a little more dense there, with gorse and bramble added to the grasses and bracken. The bramble roots made the ground uneven and perilous, and that slowed Bolan even more. He hadn't even reached a spot where he could make it across to the vines when he heard Ross's voice in his earpiece.

He'd really have to move it.

Stopping to take a full bearing, Bolan could see that he was roughly halfway around the perimeter of the estate. Looking across, he could see the roofs of both the outbuildings and the château.

Time to get across to the vines. A hundred yards or so, to be done toting the heavy combat bag. That would slow him, and even if he checked thoroughly before starting the run, this fact alone would make him more vulnerable to being spotted by any guard that may appear.

Bolan took the Beretta from its holster. It still had the sound suppressor attached. He weighted it in his palm, loosening his muscles so that he would be able to bring it up and direct a burst of fire in a fraction of a second.

He drew a breath and took one last look around. It was clear as far as he could see, and there was no sound to indicate anyone within range.

Feet pounding across the dry, barren stretch of earth, breathing deep and regular, Bolan took the empty space at a brisk pace, the Beretta ready to fire at the slightest hint of trouble. But there was none. He reached the vines without breaking a sweat.

Now to find a security patrol and take it out. He'd figured the teams were regular, but wasn't sure of their rotation. Given time, he would wait and then take them out when they passed by on their rounds, but time was the one thing he didn't have.

He'd have to flush them out. Then the burst of MP-5 fire from the far side of the estate obviated the need for that. He heard Goldman report, heard Ross retort and bit down hard on his own anger. The loud fire would attract attention, maybe spur the Chilean to use the sonic weapon to immobilize them quickly—and he still had no headset.

But if Bolan was concerned and thinking rationally about what to do and how to act, the guards were reacting rather than acting. A wry smile crossed the soldier's face as he heard some approach from the far side of the vines. He dropped the combat bag and moved stealthily toward the nearest gap in the vines. The guards were acting and thinking as though the intruders were only where the fire had sounded. They made no attempt to scout their own territory.

Bolan waited by the gap for the two guards to approach. They were almost on him when he stepped out and tapped the Beretta's trigger, the short burst of fire stopping them in their tracks and killing them before they realized they were dead. Their internal organs were pulped by the combined force of the shells, the shock trauma and the bone splinters as their chest and ribs were shattered by the blast.

Wasting no time, Bolan took a headset from one of the guards and put it on. He jumped back behind the vine and grabbed the combat bag before heading toward the château, the Beretta ready for any further intrusions.

He looked at his watch and barked into the blacksuit mike, "Attack begins in three minutes. They're rattled, so watch for them. Now lose the earpieces and get the headsets on."

He heard both Ross and Goldman acknowledge the order as he pulled out his own earpiece, letting it dangle onto his chest from its wire attachment as he pulled the headset into place.

Two minutes to get a location, set up the M-16/M-203 combo and start firing. So far there had been no other guards near him. Maybe his luck would hold.

At one minute forty-five he found his spot, a gap in the maze that would allow him a direct line at the outbuildings and the château. He dropped and opened the combat bag, taking out the pieces of the M-16 and methodically slotting them together, all the while keeping a lookout for any guards.

He had the M-203 grenade launcher in place when two guards came into view. They raised their SMGs and fired. From their faces, Bolan could see that they were panicked, and he felt splashes of earth where they were firing wide. He calmly picked up the Beretta and tapped two bursts that cut them down.

Twenty-five seconds. He loaded the M-16/M-203 combo and sighted the target.

Eight seconds. He counted until his watch hit zero, then he fired the first grenade and began to pour 5.56 mm fire at the buildings.

The attack had begun.

17

Hector Chavez-Smith was a happy man. Whatever problems had been occurring in Marseilles, he had managed to shake them off, and there had been no sign that they had been followed. Holed up in an anonymous château, there was no chance they could have been easily traced. Of course, they now had one successful test behind them, and it was a ticking clock on how long it would be before they would have the military descend on them in an attempt to find out just what had been happening, but that was unimportant.

His scientific staff of three had managed to crack the program and design of the chip much quicker than he had expected, and the test had been a success. All he needed to do now was pack up and get out, as soon as the blueprint and the first copy were complete. Attaturk—his first buyer—had stayed in Marseilles, muttering about the U.S. government being on his tail. To Chavez-Smith's cocaine paranoia, it was obvious that Attaturk was the target for the troubles. Attaturk was a barbarian, and soon Chavez-Smith would be dealing with smoother men, and with greater nations. This was the coup that would make him the greatest arms dealer in the world.

"Top of the world, Ma, top of the world," he whispered to himself as he sat in the château's study, looking out the windows onto the vineyards beyond. He sipped at the snifter of brandy in one hand, regardless of the fact that it was a time of day when brandy was not usually drunk. He looked at his watch. There would be another brief test in less than half an hour, and he had to make sure that he had the protective headset in place. It would never do for him to be caught out by his own tests. Loss of face meant more than anything.

But he didn't get the chance to make a note of the time. He was jolted from his chair by the sudden explosion on the far side of the château. It sounded like one of the outbuildings, and he'd been dealing armament long enough to know a grenade blast when he heard one. The intense chattering of an M-16 following on to the blast was all-too-familiar.

Cursing, the Chilean pulled himself out of his chair and reached the door as it was opened by one of his bodyguards.

"If you say we're under attack, then I'll fucking kill you myself," he yelled as the man opened his mouth. "You think I don't know a grenade when I hear it?"

Without another word, he moved through the corridors to the room that had been turned into an electronics lab. Opening the door, he yelled at the three people within. "Sound the preliminary. Thirty seconds and then hit the button."

It was earlier than he had hoped, but if they were under attack from the French military, then what better way to run the second weapons test but in a full combat situation?

ROSS HEARD THE FIRST explosion, then the sound of M-16 fire, and began his own advance. He moved through the maze of vines at a crouch toward the house and outbuildings. He figured that the untrained terrorists would panic. He knew from the briefing that the terrorists had been on paramilitary training in the States, but he also knew from the ease with which all three men had obtained headsets that the terrorists were slack and were not expecting trouble. Therefore, anything that happened would put them into shock for a couple of minutes. And that would be all—in theory—that they should need. Already, they had taken out six of the opposition, bringing the odds down from about ten-to-one to eight, still high, but getting better all the time.

From the direction of the buildings, he could hear shouting and confusion. Chances were, if they were to react rather than act, the terrorists would head for the direction of the fire and leave gaps for both himself and Goldman to exploit. He had grenades on his combat harness, and these would be useful for flushing the enemy from the outbuildings.

He froze as he heard voices and footsteps coming his way. They were arriving from behind him, and had to belong to an outlying security patrol that was tracking back to the château. Ross felt the sweat bead on his forehead and the small of his back. This was it.

Pivoting, he made sure that the Beretta was holstered and it was the MP-5 he was holding. In this kind of firefight, it had to be an SMG for maximum firepower.

Ross located the source of the noise. They were on the side of the vines farthest from the house, and they were heading for the nearest gap, which was about fifty yards away. Two men, a standard patrol. He had to hit them as they came through, and as they would be ready for trouble he would have to hit immediately. There would be no second chance or element of shock this time.

Ross flattened himself to the vine, trying to blot out the noise around him and concentrate only on the approaching footsteps. The guards were running and calling to each other. Calling, not speaking. One had to be a much faster runner, and had some distance on his partner. So Ross wouldn't be able to hit them both as they came through. Damn.

There was only one thing he could do. He began to move toward the gap in the vines and readied himself to fire on sight. Then, taking a deep breath, he plunged forward at the moment he judged the first guard to be near. Stepping through the gap, he tapped the trigger of the MP-5 and took out the first guard. A line of rounds tore holes in his torso from shoulder to groin, and he jerked back, his Uzi flying from his hand.

Before the body had even hit the ground, Ross ducked to his left, cannoning into the vine to avoid return fire from the other guard. The higher pitched chatter of the guard's Uzi cut through the noise that seemed to fill the previously silent vineyard, deafeningly loud in the merc's ears. The leaves on the vine deadened some of the sound, and wrapped themselves around his face as he sank into them, making it hard to get a clear sight of the man firing at him. Panic welled up as he realized he may get himself killed before he had a chance to return fire, and his finger tightened on the MP-5's trigger, squeezing off another burst. He heard a scream as the body hit the ground.

The second guard had dropped his Uzi. The wild shots from the blinded Ross had chopped into the guard's legs, leaving his kneecaps and shins shattered, and he had sunk down, unable to support his own weight. Trying desperately to stand, or at least to scramble for where his SMG had landed, the man was temporarily out of the action. He saw Ross come back out of the vines, MP-5 raised. There was a desperate, imploring look in his eyes as Ross caught sight of them, but there was no time to show mercy. Ross tapped the trigger and sent the guard backward in an awkward, spastic motion as the momentum of the bullets propelled him.

It was then that Ross heard the siren, cutting through the noise of battle. His brow furrowed for a fraction of a second before it hit him. A warning that the sonic weapon was about to be deployed. It made sense to use it, as Chavez-Smith would figure they had no defense against this weapon, and however many of them there were could then be easily mopped up by his forces.

Oh, how wrong you are, Ross thought as pulled the protective headset into place. Immediately, the noise of battle was replaced by a soothing white noise that was at a moderate volume. This had to be the frequency blocker. It did give him one problem. How could he hear the enemy approach with this in his ears?

Then he smiled. If he had this problem, then so did Chavez-Smith's private army. The odds were leveled on that score, at least.

Grinning to himself, and moving forward with much more caution now that he had to rely solely on his eyes, Ross turned back and moved through the vines, heading for the château.

GOLDMAN HAD ALLOWED himself to grin. The sound of the detonated grenades followed by the chatter of 5.56 mm ammo being unleashed had stirred his blood. He began to move toward the château through the cover of the vineyards. His teeth were still bared in a grin, but of a more vulpine nature, when he sighted the two guards coming at him. One had an Uzi, but the other was carrying an AKSU assault rifle. Goldman, with his MP-5, was on the lookout for the terrorists, whereas they were still confused about what was going on and not fully alert.

That was the last error either of them would make. A woman was holding the Uzi, and before she had time to take a bead on Goldman he had drilled a line across her chest and abdomen with one swift tap on the MP-5's trigger. As she was thrown backward, she let loose a useless burst of Uzi fire into the air. She crashed to the ground, dead.

Goldman threw himself down and to his left as he fired, making it hard for the left-handed man with the AKSU to bring the weapon around and down in order to take aim. This was exactly what Goldman had intended, as it bought him the time to resight the MP-5 and tap the trigger once more. Another short, controlled burst took out the struggling terrorist with a line that zipped straight from his crotch to his throat. He dropped the AKSU as he hit the ground without even firing it.

Goldman sprang to his feet. Certainly, he felt confidant that if this was the best that Destiny's Spear and Hector Chavez-Smith could do, then the element of surprise should give them enough of an edge to beat the odds and take the terrorists out.

He began to move forward rapidly, keeping an eye out for movement. It was then that he heard the alarm. He furrowed his brow, momentarily puzzled, before realizing that it had to signal the beginning of the test. He grinned again. That stupid Chilean hadn't thought that they might have taken some headsets already, he thought.

He pulled the headset into place, securing it over his ears. He tapped it. There was nothing coming through. Maybe the blocking frequency didn't cut in until the weapon was actually in use.

Worried by the lack of any sound at all in his headset, Goldman turned and backtracked to where he had left the dead terrorists. Hurrying as he knew now that time was of the essence, he ripped off the headset and sank onto one knee to take a set off one of the corpses. As he lifted it up, he could hear a faint sound coming from the set, like the static on an untuned TV set.

Dammit, trust him to pick up the only headset on the whole damned estate that had been damaged, he thought. He tugged the headset away from the corpse's head, but it snagged, and he had to pull again.

He became aware of a nagging ache in both ears. It was like an itch deep inside, no, like a pain. He screamed. It was like a wasp had stung him on each eardrum. The agony was intense and yet also exquisite.

Goldman became aware that the world was moving away from him, as if it were something that he was watching on a movie screen, a photograph, garish and only two dimensional. It was hard to think, impossible to move.

BOLAN WATCHED THE outbuilding explode as the grenades hit. The 5.56 mm ammo he had poured onto the site was also doing some serious damage. But the time had come for him to stop the long-distance bombardment and move in for the kill. He slipped the magazine from the M-16 and left it standing temporarily useless. Unslinging his AKSU and taking a grenade from the combat harness on the blacksuit, Bolan began to run toward the house. It was then that he heard the alarm begin to sound.

Pulling the pin from the grenade and holding the spoon down while he drew back his arm, he then let the spoon free and tossed the grenade in a high arc over the vines toward the outbuildings. He then stopped to pull the headset into place.

But first he yelled into the blacksuit's mike, "Jack, they're about to start the weapon. You and Walters stop monitoring now."

"But Sarge—" Grimaldi began.

"No, Jack! Stop now and wait until you hear from me. Just monitor the perimeters."

"Okay," Grimaldi agreed reluctantly.

Bolan took the earpiece for the blacksuit transmitter out

of his ear and pulled the headset into place. The sound of white noise took over, and he found that all other sound disappeared. This would make advancing difficult, as he would be unable to hear any approaches. On the other hand, the terrorists wouldn't be expecting the attack to continue.

Moving forward, he saw rather than heard the grenade explode. One side of a barn began to collapse, the last explosion being the one necessary to bring down the edifice. With any luck, it may have taken out a few terrorists.

It was strange to see the explosion and feel the ground shaking under his feet as he ran, but not actually hear it. However, he put the feeling to one side. He would need to be a hundred percent focused if he was going to pull this one off.

The twisting maze of vines now became a death run. Unable to hear the approach of an enemy, Bolan had to move swiftly through the tangle of vines without anyone getting the drop on him. The sooner he was past this point, the sooner he would be able to get a full, panoramic view of the target area. Right now, the enemy could appear around the corner at any second, and he would be caught cold.

At some points, the thickness of the cover provided by the grapes and the large leaves of the vines thinned out enough for him to be able to see through to the other side, and judge if there was any opposition in a position to hit him. It was only as he tackled the last hole in the wall of the vines that he felt it safe to assume that the terrorists had pulled back in order to defend the strongholds of the remaining outbuilding, and the château itself. They would be hoping that the sonic attack had taken effect, but were also unsure about how many soldiers they were facing.

As Bolan pulled up by the opening that would lead him into the open courtyard area at the side of the château, he was also wondering the same thing. He had no way of knowing if Ross and Goldman had been successful in avoiding the guards and the sonic attack, and if they were on their way.

ERROL ROSS FACED the rear of the château. He was crouched by the opening, surveying the damage ahead. The windows at the rear of the building had all been blown out, and there was some damage to the upper floors of the three-story structure. One of the outbuildings had the large double doors blown out, and had some structural damage, including a section of the roof caved in. The other outbuilding had collapsed on itself, leaving it little more than a heap of rubble from which dust and some smoke were still rising, a small fire visible in what remained of the central section. Three dead terrorists were in the rear courtyard, and he could see some arms and legs poking out of the rubble.

Already, it looked as though the initial assault had gone some way toward evening the odds. Ross sat back on his heels and pondered the best course of action. The standing outbuilding could house some terrorists that would have to be neutralized. But the chances were that the terrorists had pulled back into the château, to establish one strong base rather than splitting their resources. Also, he felt sure that Chavez-Smith would have contingency plans to pull them back, as defense of the chip had to be his priority.

So, before tackling the house, he had to just make sure that the outbuilding posed no threat. There was only one way to do that. He took two grenades from his combat harness and pulled the pin on the first. From a position that would enable him to stand upright, getting a good angle on the outbuilding and yet not be seen from the château, he swung back his arm and lobbed the grenade toward the outbuilding. It went into the open double doors. Before it had a chance to detonate, he

had taken the pin from the second and thrown that bomb in
a higher trajectory, tossing it into an opening on the upper
floor that had once been used to heft sacks of grain into the
top story, as the pulley mechanism still attached to the wall
attested. Ross then dived across the opening in the vines and
rolled to cover, watching the grapes splatter into a blood colored pulp as SMG fire from the château followed the arc of
the grenades back to the source. He backed into the vines,
watching the dirt in front of him being kicked up by the shells
as they bit into the ground where the terrorists thought he was
lying.

The explosions sounded close enough to each other to be
almost one, not that he could hear it through the white noise
in his ears, but he could feel the earth beneath him shake as
from the explosions and then the aftershock as the outbuilding collapsed in on itself.

All the surviving terrorist forces would be concentrated in
the château now, he was certain of that.

And all he had to do was get past them.

BOLAN HAD A SIXTH SENSE about danger, born of many long
missions—which was why he suddenly hit the ground behind
the cover of the vines a fraction of a second before he felt the
earth shake beneath him from the double explosion.

So at least one of his partners was still in the game. A rain
of debris showered about him, none of it large enough to
cause injury, but proof enough of the grenades' success. As
the soldier pulled himself to his feet, he readied the AKSU
for a charge on the château. From his position, the rubble
would provide adequate cover. He just hoped that whoever
had thrown the grenades was satisfied with his work, and

didn't want to lob one more to make sure while he was in the area.

Bolan came out of cover and raced for the debris. Nothing could live in that carnage, and the attention of the terrorists would be focused on the direction of the attack. If he moved fast and kept low, he should be able to avoid detection. There would be a watch on this side of the château, but as there was still so much dust and confusion he may be able to move without being seen.

He attained cover without a shot pocking the earth around him, and from his position behind a mound of brick and splintered wood, he looked at the west side of the château. Several windows were at ground level, all of which had been blown out by the proximity to the blast. They looked deserted, as though the terrorists guarding them had pulled back at the explosions.

Perhaps they had. If the electronics facility of the château was situated on another side of the building, then maybe Chavez-Smith would pull the guards back to defend it until he was in a position to get away with the hardware.

But how would he do this? Bolan found it hard to believe that a hardened criminal and terrorist sympathizer like the Chilean would rely only on the roads. He would have a chopper on call, surely? But then, how would he call it up without killing the sonic weapon?

And by now, all the enemy fighters had to have realized that whoever was attacking had headsets that also protected them. Would this mean that the weapon had been stopped to facilitate an escape?

There was no way that the soldier could tell this without risking himself. He had to get inside the château. If the terrorists had discarded their headsets he could discard his, but until that time, he would be at a disadvantage.

Damn, it could have been going better.

Ross pumped MP-5 fire into the windows at the rear of the château. The ground-floor door at the back was open, and the muzzle-flash of an SMG told him that there were guards stationed there. If he could knock them out, then he may have an entry. He stopped firing, and with a smooth fluid motion changed magazines. Right now, he could do with his partners taking some action and getting the heat off him.

He started to fire sparingly, waiting to try to catch the guards as they entered the window frames and doorway for the split second it took to fire. It was getting tedious. They had him pinned down, and there was no way he could knock them all out, even if he stood there from now until Christmas. He needed another edge.

There were three grenades left on the harness, as all three men had been allotted five. If he lobbed one into the château's back entrance, he was taking the risk of blocking his own means of entry. But so what? Was he going to stand there all day and get fired at?

Ross pulled a grenade, removed the pin and sent the egg sailing through the air.

It pitched just short of the building, and rolled up against the wall between the back door and one of the shattered windows. He watched as a terrorist, shouting something that couldn't be heard above the white noise in his ears, jumped out of the doorway and tried to scoop the grenade, probably to try and lob it back in his direction.

It was a stupid move. There was no way the man had enough time to try anything so foolhardy. His hand had just brushed the grenade, prior to closing and picking it up, when the egg detonated. Ross looked away from the flash, hugging the ground as it shook. When he looked up again through a gap in the vines, he could see that there was nothing left of the terrorist beyond a smear of flesh and bone fragments. Neither was there a door nor a window. Instead, a gaping hole revealed how tenuous the outer brickwork had been. One thing for sure—this had forced the terrorists back into the house, and—taking a deep breath to steel himself—Ross ran from cover, zigzagging as he headed fast and low for the entrance to the château.

He dived through the doorway, rolling as he did, and coming up with the MP-5 arcing around. He was safe. The guards that hadn't either perished or lost their headsets and so become paralyzed by the sonic attack, had pulled back farther into the house.

Now all he had to do was find his way around.

A PUFF OF SMOKE and a tremor from the rear of the building told Bolan that there was some action. It could be just the distraction he needed. Spraying some exploratory fire from the AKSU at the bare window openings, he noted that there was no sign of return fire, no kicked up dust and dirt, no ricochets from the collapsed brickwork around him. He surveyed the open portals. No sign of any life whatsoever.

Deciding that it was a risk worth taking, Bolan rose to his feet and charged over the rubble, surefooted among the shifting debris as he made his way toward the western side of the château. As he reached the line of broken ground-floor windows, he selected one and dived through it, coming up and spraying a short burst of fire, in order to secure his position. Although there were no guards in view when he had the opportunity to look, there was no way he could call it a waste of ammo. With his ears useless for the duration, he could take no chances.

The soldier tried to recall the layout of the château in his mind. He had seen a plan of it before they left the airfield, and if he could remember anything, it may prove to be useful. He was on the western side. If he was right, the larger rooms were at the front, on the northern side. The Chilean would need one of the larger rooms to use as an electronics lab, and chances were that it would be secured on an upper floor, out of the way of casual visitors. There may not have been many, but it only took one suspicious tradesman or a gendarme on his rounds. The Chilean was too canny to fall into that trap.

So Chavez-Smith would want the front, and an upper floor. Bolan headed to the northern side of the building, keeping his eyes open for the slightest sign of movement.

The question was, how many of the opposition had they eliminated?

ROSS MOVED through the interior of the château at ground-floor level, finding it deserted. Where had all the terrorists gone? He'd covered the south and east of the château, so they had to be either on the west side, or on an upper floor. Why would they be up there? Strategically, it was the dumbest move they could make. The high ground was only good when someone was outdoors. All they were doing in the château was cutting themselves off from any avenue of escape. Unless...

How could he be so dumb? The whole base of operations had to work out of an upstairs room, and the Chilean had pulled them back to protect it. So if it was so empty downstairs, did it mean there weren't many terrorists left?

Things were starting to look good. At least until he came to the large, ornate hall that served the imposing double doors of the château's entrance. As soon as Ross's shadow was visible, he was greeted by a hail of SMG fire that made him pull back.

But before he did, he caught sight of something that made him feel a little more optimistic. On the far side of the hall he could see his partner—who was signaling him.

BOLAN SAW Ross draw back as the gunfire rained down, and he hoped the merc had seen him. An answering hand signal affirmed it. There was no sign of Goldman, but at least they could now work a two-pronged attack on the upstairs.

Like all buildings of that age and design, there had to be another way onto the upper floor besides the large, sweeping staircase. But time was of the essence, and the chances were that there were still enough guards to cover those. No, the only way to get this resolved before they became entrenched was to make a full-frontal assault. There had been no gunfire aimed at the Executioner as he approached the hall, so it was reasonable to assume the guards were only aware of Ross's presence.

Bolan gestured to Ross, asking how many grenades the man had left. Ross held up two fingers. Bolan gestured to himself and held up four. Okay, so they had more than enough power to blow a hole through the upstairs and cause confusion. The only drawback was this kind of attack would also take out the staircase itself, and leave them with the problem of having to find an alternative means of access.

Only one way to find out for certain. Indicating to Ross that he should draw the guards' fire, Bolan took two grenades from his combat harness. As the merc held his MP-5 around the door and fired a random burst, inviting a flurry of return fire, Bolan pulled the pin from the first grenade and tossed the bomb underhand so that it landed at the top of the staircase, rolling along the hallway beyond. Before it had even touched down, he had pulled the pin on the second grenade and tossed the lethal egg onto the other side of the staircase.

Ross and Bolan both drew back, waiting for the tremor that would signal the blast. The château shook under the force of the twin attack, plaster showering from the ceiling as the structure of the house creaked and gave under the stress of the blast.

Both men put their weapons around the angle of their respective hiding places and fired a burst. There was nothing in return.

Looking around the doorway, Bolan could see the staircase was still intact, although the hallway on either side was a mass of rubble, perhaps with an unsafe floor. There was no sign of any guards other than those who had been killed by the blast.

Glancing across, he caught Ross's eye. Indicating that they should advance, both men came out of hiding and took the stairs a section at a time, one taking point for the other, until they had reached the top.

Ross signaled, asking which direction?

Bolan indicated that he would take the left while Ross took the right. He then held his hand palm down, gesturing slowly as if to say take it easy. Ross gave him a grin and nodded.

There were several doorways extending along each wing of the château, but there was no need for them to waste time exploring.

The Destiny's Spear guards gave themselves away in their panic.

Before the two men had even parted, two guards appeared from a doorway on the left-hand side, firing indiscriminately. Bolan saw them. Ross had already turned away, but the Executioner pushed him in the back, pitching him forward, out of the line of fire.

Ross realized what had happened before he hit the ground, the wooden flooring kicking up splinters in front of him as the rounds hit home. He rolled and brought up the MP-5, tapping off a burst of return fire to accompany the soldier's measured fire from the AKSU. Bolan had sunk to one knee and was firing off shots that took out the guards, and drove any further opposition back into their defensive positions.

Ross now joined Bolan, and they began to advance along the corridor past the rubble, using the shelter of the unoccupied rooms to provide cover for each advance. They moved in a step formation, one covering the other as they moved. Within a matter of seconds they were on the verge of taking the electronics lab.

It was situated in one room at the end of the corridor, facing the front of the building. Bolan indicated to Ross to cover him, then pitched himself across the closed doorway so that they now stood one on each side.

They paused, unsure of what was happening. Unable to hear any sounds from behind the closed and—presumably—barricaded door, it was impossible to know how to tackle to situation.

Bolan took a grenade from his combat harness, but was stopped by Ross's frantic gesturing. Bolan gave him a quizzical look, and Ross indicated his ears.

Bolan put the grenade back in his webbing and mouthed "What?" at the mercenary. Ross returned with a gesture that he would kick the door in if Bolan covered him.

The Executioner was appalled. Ross was taking a hugely unnecessary risk to recover the sonic chip. He shook his head, but the man was insistent. Bolan shrugged. What could he do to stop Ross?

Ross stepped back and lifted a foot before crashing it against the door.

It was the last thing he ever did. When the Chilean's guards had barred the door to the electronics lab, they had booby-trapped it. As Ross's foot crashed against the wood, it triggered a small, armed explosive device that exploded, throwing Ross backward against the wall, his leg missing at the calf, blood pouring from the wound and from contusions and cuts caused by large splinters of wood. One had gouged a hole in his throat, and his life blood was pumping out in time with his leg wound.

Bolan had flung himself away from the explosion, and was spared all except a few lights before the eyes from the flash of the blast. He scrambled to his feet and, taking one look at Ross and realizing that there was nothing he could do to help the merc, he took a grenade and pulled the pin, releasing the spoon as he threw it into the room.

The upper floor of the château shook, part of the corridor wall collapsing as the blast tore through the enclosed space. Bolan waited for the dust to settle and stepped into the room, assault rifle at the ready.

Inside was carnage. The electronics lab had been well-insulated, and the insulation had allowed little of the fragmentation to escape. The walls and the shattered equipment were covered with shards of metal. All the working equipment was burned out, and there was little left of the people who had been sheltering within. Bolan recognized what was left of Hector Chavez-Smith, and figured on seven other people whose remains were scattered.

The white noise in his ears had stopped. Bolan took off the headset and listened to the almost deafening silence. If there was anyone else left standing in the château, they were staying quiet.

The Executioner walked slowly across the room, listening to the creaking floorboards, and the moaning of a structure that was almost shattered beyond repair. He'd better get out as soon as possible. But first…

It took only a few moments to find what he was looking for. The transmission device. The computer itself was broken, but the chip, attached externally, was still intact. In a small box next to it sat another. The original and the copy.

Bolan took them both, dropped them on the floor and crushed them beneath his heel. For this, more than fifty people had died in the past few days. A product of a black project culture in the U.S. military that stood contrary to everything Bolan believed about America. Maybe the man in the Oval Office would have liked these. Oh well. The black project also had the plans for the chip and would no doubt make it again.

Bolan had managed to delay them for at least a little while.

He checked that the chips were beyond repair, then pondered his next problem. If Grimaldi had switched off the blacksuit mike transmitter, then how was he going to contact him? Suddenly he turned to the corpse of Hector Chavez-Smith, a fragment of steel embedded in the center of his forehead, his eyes still surprised. Bolan searched him and found a cell phone. It was still working. Bolan tapped in a number and waited.

"Hello?" Grimaldi said tentatively.

"It's me, Jack," Bolan replied. "Come and get me out. Ross is dead, so is Goldman, I think. That Chilean scumbag certainly is. So's everyone else as far as I can tell. I've destroyed the chip."

"I figure it's mission accomplished. I'll be with you in five."

Epilogue

Bolan left the château and walked across the vineyards to where the decommissioned M-16/M-203 combo and the combat bag lay waiting for him. Although he was pretty sure he was the only one left standing after the assault, he still cradled the AKSU, ready to fire if the need arose. He looked back at the crumbling remains of the outbuildings and the Château Soleil, which was looking pretty much of a wreck itself.

Another round in the War Everlasting was over. This time the good guys had won. He took a look around before starting to dismantle the combo. He would have to put down the AKSU while he packed the heavier gun away, and there was something nagging at him, something that wasn't quite right. All the while he dismantled the large assault rifle, he kept looking around. But there was no movement or sound that would justify his nagging doubt.

With the combat bag packed, Bolan picked it up, then shouldered the AKSU and began to walk into the middle of the land between the wilderness and the vines.

"Come on, Jack, or else the French military will be asking me some damned awkward questions," he said softly, watching the skies and listening for Grimaldi's approach. They would have to go back in and get Ross's corpse before they could leave. A man in a blacksuit would take a little too much explaining, and Hal Brognola wouldn't be happy about it.

It was while he was looking up that he became aware of something in the corner of his eye—a figure, staggering out from the vines away to the eastern side. Bolan dropped the bag and drew the Beretta. The figure seemed too unsteady to be any threat, but nonetheless…

As Bolan settled his gaze on the figure, he was astounded to see that it was Goldman. Bolan holstered the Beretta and moved slowly toward the staggering man. He halted when the dazed mercenary lifted his MP-5 and directed it at him.

"Hold it! Don't move," Goldman commanded, his voice was slurred and as unsteady as his gait. He seemed to be carrying no obvious injuries, and Bolan could only surmise for some reason that he had failed to use his headset in time.

"Goldman, Jimmy Goldman," Bolan called in a firm, clear voice. "Do you remember why you're here?"

Even at this distance, he could see the frown cross Goldman's face. Bolan held his hands up above his head to signal his intent, and his lack of hardware to hand.

"I remember a lot of things, but not why I'm here. And not you," Goldman said threateningly.

"Look at yourself," Bolan continued, ignoring the implied hostility. "You're wearing a blacksuit, like me. Like your partner. And you came here with me. You've sustained a psychological injury in the course of combat."

"Where's Errol?" Goldman cut across Bolan's attempted explanation.

Bolan hesitated. How the hell could he tell Goldman that Ross was dead without the hotheaded mercenary losing it?

"Ross has sustained something far worse," he said awkwardly.

Goldman let the MP-5 fall. "Worse? If he's not with you…" Suddenly he pulled the SMG upright again, and his voice took on a harder tone. "If he's dead, then you're going to have to explain yourself a bit better than you have."

"He's dead," the Executioner stated. "I wish I could tell you otherwise. He died in the line of duty."

"Duty? What does that mean?" Goldman spit. "We don't work for any army. We—"

"You're mercenaries, and you were employed to carry out this operation with myself and my colleague, who's flying in to pick us up now," Bolan interjected hurriedly. "We have to get the hell out of here. We were successful, but the French military will be down on us soon, and I don't think we want to be answering any awkward questions they may care to put to us," he continued. It wasn't exactly the truth, but it would serve until he had the time to debrief the confused merc.

"Why would the French military want us?" Goldman asked, genuinely puzzled.

"Because we're in France," Bolan answered flatly, not knowing what else to say. It occurred to him that the black ops people who had employed Goldman and Ross would have a field day studying the surviving merc if they got their hands on him. If he remembered as much as the locals who had previously been affected, then he'd lost a year of his life. Bolan resolved that he would enlist the help of Stony Man and Brognola to insure that Goldman was helped.

Goldman had stayed silent on hearing this, looking even

more confused, as though trying to work it out in his head, which was already scrambled enough.

But then he looked up. Like Bolan, he had heard the approach of Grimaldi's chopper. The big black bird was closing in on them fast.

"That's our ticket out," Bolan yelled. "You want to come back to the house and help me get Ross's body? The least he deserves is a proper burial."

Somehow, this idea snapped Goldman out of his confused reverie. He looked blankly at Bolan and nodded, putting away the MP-5 and following the Executioner back to the château.

Mounting the dangerously damaged staircase, they picked their way among the debris and the bodies in the house until they came to the spot where Errol Ross lay in a pool of his own blood, his leg severed at the calf and the splinter still stuck in his throat.

For a moment, Bolan thought that Goldman was going to vomit, but instead the redhead pulled the splinter free and tossed it away. He bent down and gently picked up the body of his dead partner.

"You need a hand?" Bolan asked.

Goldman shot him a glance underscored with menace. "No, I'll do it," he said in a monotone.

Bolan allowed him to carry the corpse down the staircase and out of the château. They took the front entrance, where the double doors were blast-damaged but still secure, and walked around the perimeter of the vineyard to where Grimaldi had set down the chopper. The pilot appeared in the hatch, and although Goldman tried to shrug off the pilot's attempts to assist him, he eventually had to let the pilot help him up into the chopper. Bolan watched, then picked up the combat bag and jumped up into the belly of the aircraft.

"What's with him?" Grimaldi whispered as Bolan joined him. "He didn't seem to know who I was."

"He doesn't know, Jack. He doesn't know anything about the mission. He wasn't wearing a headset. I don't know why. But I do know that he's grieving for his partner, and someone is going to have to do a lot of explaining to him before he can work out just what he's been through."

"Yeah, but at least he's still alive," Grimaldi said.

Bolan gave a single shake of his head. "You know, I'm not sure he's so pleased about that right now. Come on, Jack, we need to get out of here. Can Walters cover the air traces before the French move in?"

Grimaldi shrugged. "He's a bright boy, Sarge. He'll manage. The question is, how are you going to explain this to Hal? He's going to have to account for this to the man in the Oval Office. It was only supposed to be a quiet little covert operation."

"Hal's the least of our problems. And he'll square things with the Man. He always does," he added wearily, then he settled himself into his seat as Grimaldi lifted the bird off the ground, heading for home.

Stony Man is deployed against an armed
invasion on American soil...

TERMS OF CONTROL

Supertankers bound for the U.S. are being sabotaged,
and key foreign enterprises in America are coming under
attack. The message is loud and clear: someone wants the
U.S. to close its borders to outsiders—and Stony Man thinks
it knows who...a powerful senator bringing his own brand
of isolationism to the extreme. He's hired mercenaries to
do the dirty work, and the body toll is rising by the hour.
The outcome all boils down to luck, timing and the
combat skills of a few good men....

STONY MAN®

*Available
June 2004
at your favorite
retail outlet.*

Or order your copy now by sending your name, address, zip or postal code, along with
a check or money order (please do not send cash) for $6.50 for each book ordered
($7.99 in Canada), plus 75¢ postage and handling ($1.00 in Canada), payable to Gold
Eagle Books, to:

In the U.S.	In Canada
Gold Eagle Books	Gold Eagle Books
3010 Walden Avenue	P.O. Box 636
P.O. Box 9077	Fort Erie, Ontario
Buffalo, NY 14269-9077	L2A 5X3

Please specify book title with your order.
Canadian residents add applicable federal and provincial taxes.

GOLD EAGLE®

GSM71

James Axler
Outlanders

SUN LORD

In a fabled city of the ancient world, the neo-gods of Mexico are locked in a battle for domination. Harnessing the immutable power of alien technology and Earth's pre-Dark secrets, the high priests and whitecoats have hijacked Kane into the resurrected world of the Aztecs. Invested with the power of the great sun god, Kane is a pawn in the brutal struggle and must restore the legendary Quetzalcoatl to his rightful place—or become a human sacrifice....

Available May 2004 at your favorite retail outlet.

Or order your copy now by sending your name, address, zip or postal code, along with a check or money order (please do not send cash) for $6.50 for each book ordered ($7.99 in Canada), plus 75¢ postage and handling ($1.00 in Canada), payable to Gold Eagle Books, to:

In the U.S.	In Canada
Gold Eagle Books	Gold Eagle Books
3010 Walden Avenue	P.O. Box 636
P.O. Box 9077	Fort Erie, Ontario
Buffalo, NY 14269-9077	L2A 5X3

Please specify book title with your order.
Canadian residents add applicable federal and provincial taxes.

GOLD EAGLE

GOUT29

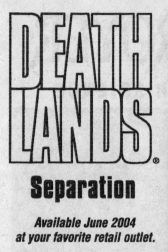

DEATH LANDS.

Separation

Available June 2004
at your favorite retail outlet.

The group makes its way to a remote island in hopes of finding brief sanctuary. Instead, they are captured by an isolated tribe of descendants of African slaves from pre–Civil War days. When they declare Mildred Wyeth "free" from her white masters, it is a twist of fate that ultimately leads the battle-hardened medic to question where her true loyalties lie. Will she side with Ryan, J. B. Dix and those with whom she has forged a bond of trust and friendship…or with the people of her own blood?

Or order your copy now by sending your name, address, zip or postal code, along with a check or money order (please do not send cash) for $6.50 for each book ordered ($7.99 in Canada), plus 75¢ postage and handling ($1.00 in Canada), payable to Gold Eagle Books, to:

In the U.S.	In Canada
Gold Eagle Books	Gold Eagle Books
3010 Walden Ave.	P.O. Box 636
P.O. Box 9077	Fort Erie, Ontario
Buffalo, NY 14269-9077	L2A 5X3

Please specify book title with order.
Canadian residents add applicable federal and provincial taxes.

GDL66

THE DESTROYER

UNPOPULAR SCIENCE

A rash of perfectly executed thefts from military research facilities puts CURE in the hot seat, setting the trap for Remo and Chiun to flip the off switch of the techno-genius behind an army of remote-controlled killer machines. Nastier than a scourge of deadly titanium termites, more dangerous than the resurrection of a machine oil/microchip battle-bot called Ironhand, is the juice used to power them all up: an electromagnetic pulse that can unplug Remo and Chiun long enough to short-circuit CURE beyond repair.

Available July 2004 at your favorite retail outlet.

Or order your copy now by sending your name, address, zip or postal code, along with a check or money order (please do not send cash) for $6.50 for each book ordered ($7.99 in Canada), plus 75¢ postage and handling ($1.00 in Canada), payable to Gold Eagle Books, to:

In the U.S.	In Canada
Gold Eagle Books	Gold Eagle Books
3010 Walden Avenue	P.O. Box 636
P.O. Box 9077	Fort Erie, Ontario
Buffalo, NY 14269-9077	L2A 5X3

Please specify book title with your order.
Canadian residents add applicable federal and provincial taxes.

GOLD EAGLE ®

GDEST136